The Ghost is Clear

THE GHOST DETECTIVE MYSTERIES - BOOK 3

JANE HINCHEY

· BP ·
BAYWOLF PRESS
BAYWOLF PRESS

AUTHOR'S NOTE

Hey! Welcome to the weird and wacky world of my imagination. I hope you enjoy your time here.

If you love anything supernatural as much as I do, then you're going to enjoy the journey ahead - at least I think you will.

Give up the Ghost is the second book in my Ghost Detective series, with more to come, so make sure you sign up for my newsletter to get notifications on when the next book is ready.

You can sign up for my newsletter here:
Janehinchey.com/subscribe

Okay, ready to weave some magic and solve some mysteries?

I'll see you on the other side!

xoxo

Jane

ABOUT THIS BOOK

Amateur sleuth, PI in training, ghost whisperer.

That's me. Audrey Fitzgerald, ghost detective. I'm finally coming to terms with the fact that I can not only communicate with ghosts, but animals too. Well, one in particular, my big grey teddy bear of a cat, Thor. What I haven't worked out yet is how to keep my newfound abilities a secret from the townsfolk of Firefly Bay.

When I'm hired by the president of the local historical society to find a missing necklace, I figured I finally had a case that didn't require ghostly interference. After all, how hard could it be to find a missing piece of jewelry? Things turn complicated real fast when the necklace turns up in the most unexpected of places and my client turns up dead.

Now I'm up to my neck in ghostly chatter, I have a murder to solve, my PI exams are looming, I'm worried I may have to put Thor on a diet, and I think I've accidentally fallen for Captain Cowboy Hot Pants— aka, Detective Kade Galloway. But worst of all? What on earth do I put on my business card without scaring off the townsfolk? Amateur sleuth, PI in training, ghost whisperer, or ghost detective?

Join Audrey Fitzgerald in the Ghost Detective series, a

romantic paranormal cozy mystery featuring a talking cat, a ghost, and a murder to solve.

CHAPTER ONE

Sexy. Edgy. Refined. Three words I don't normally associate with myself, but today I'd nailed it. I'd channeled Jane Bond to perfection. Smoothing my hands over the curves of my black fitted dress, I admired my reflection in the full-length mirror in the ladies' bathroom of the Firefly Bay Museum, twisting this way and that to check all angles. The dress was a classic. Knee-length, demure neckline, sleeveless.

My blonde hair was pulled back into a French twist, only it wasn't long enough, so I had over a hundred bobby pins holding it in place. My scalp was already protesting, but I ignored the discomfort. Jane Bond would not be complaining about a few hairpins.

On my feet, black patent stilettos, legs encased in twenty denier pantyhose. A bold gesture on my behalf, since me and pantyhose do not play well together. But I was on a case, and desperate times call for desperate measures.

Opening the evening purse hooked over my elbow, I pulled out my Chanel lipstick and re-coated my lips in 99 Pirate red, smacking them together with a popping noise before sliding the lipstick back into my purse. Clasping my palms together and extending my index fingers, I aimed my mock gun at my reflection, shot off two rounds before blowing the smoke from my fingertips with the perfect pout.

"Jane Bond, I presume?" Ben asked, appearing behind me.

"Eeeek!" I dropped my fake gun and felt a blush of color sweep over my cheeks. Not that I had anything to be embarrassed about. Ben was a ghost, and I was the only one who could see or hear him. Therefore, who was he going to tell that I'd been fooling around in the bathroom?

I preened some more in the mirror, admired the black sweeping winged eyeliner one last time before turning to the door. "Did you find our client?" I asked.

"Err. Audrey?"

I stopped and looked up at the ceiling. I knew that tone. The tone that warned me I would not like what he had to say next.

"What?"

"You have a run in your pantyhose."

"Of course I do." I sighed. It was a given, I knew I was challenging the Gods by putting on sheer tights, but I'd decided to risk it and go all in. "Where?"

"Back left leg, just above the ankle."

"Is it really noticeable?" I briefly wondered if I could ignore it, pretend it didn't exist, but Ben dashed all hopes.

"Oh yeah. What did you do, stick your thumb through it? Runs all the way up under your skirt."

"It's a dress, not a skirt," I grumbled. Flinging my purse onto the countertop, I hiked up the hem of my dress, then stopped and shot a look at my best friend. "Turn around."

He laughed and did as instructed. "You are such a disaster, Audrey Fitzgerald."

Wriggling out of the pantyhose, I wadded them in a ball and tossed them in the trash. The thing was, Ben wasn't wrong. I was the clumsiest person I knew, and tonight I'd known the risk I was taking, not only with the pantyhose but the stilettos. But I was on a case. The risk was more than worth it.

"So?" I prompted Ben as I picked up my purse. "Did you spot our client?"

"I did." Ben glanced over his shoulder, and upon seeing I was decent, turned around. "Anita Finley is in attendance."

"Good." I nodded. "Then let's get to it and find the missing diamond necklace."

Ben snorted. "It's hardly the crown jewels, Fitz. You're making it sound like it's this priceless necklace encrusted with diamonds. It's a single pendant with more sentimental value than monetary value."

"On a gold chain. Therefore, a diamond necklace."

"I think you're making more of this than there is. She said herself the clasp was faulty. It probably came undone and fell off without her noticing. It could be anywhere."

"Mrs. Finley believes it was stolen and hired Delaney Investigations to find it." I brushed past him, ignoring the icy chill that danced over my arm where we touched. "And find it, I shall." I pushed down the niggling worry that this entire case smacked of the proverbial needle in a haystack.

Stepping out of the bathroom, I turned right through the glass doors into the museum. Added to the eighteen seventy stone cottage that had started as a firehouse and was now home to Firefly's Historical Society, of which my client, Anita Finley, was president. The museum itself was a modern wing, all glass and chrome. And tonight was the museum's annual dinner.

Ben, who was walking alongside me with silent footsteps, had a smirk on his face. I didn't like it when Ben smirked. It usually meant something was up. Something I wouldn't like.

"What?"

"Have you ever been to one of these before, Fitz?" he asked, head cocked.

I shrugged. "No. Why's that?"

"Oh, nothing, nothing. Please." He stood aside and waved an arm. "Go right on in."

Shaking my head, I made my way through the foyer of the museum and into the main event. I'd been expecting waiters with trays of canapes, women in evening attire, and men in suits. What I got was a wooden trestle table laden with potluck dinners, anything from spaghetti to pinwheel sandwiches, paper plates, and Dixie cups, and about twenty people milling around, plates piled high. Their attire consisted mostly of T-shirts and cotton blouses, the odd flash of tweed, and an abundance of denim.

"Well, this is just peachy." I gritted through my teeth, plastering on a smile and heading toward Anita Finley, who was in conversation with Keagan Dunn. Keagan was the owner of the Artistic Affair Gallery next door and vice president of the historical society, and yet despite that, he was most pleasing to look at. I pegged him to be in his late thirties, early forties, with a head of thick brown hair that stood up in several directions and could use a good cut, clean-shaven, dark-framed glasses giving him a geeky appeal.

"Why, Audrey." Anita looked me up and down. "Don't you look lovely."

I smiled weakly and ran a hand over my stomach. "Overdressed is more like it."

Keagan looked me up and down, giving me a thorough inspection before he raised his gaze to meet my eyes. I didn't miss the gleam of appreciation in them. "If only more women took pride in their appearance. You look beautiful." Before I could stop him, he'd taken my hand and bestowed a kiss on the back of it. I blinked in surprise.

"Err. Thank you." I eased my hand from his grip and resisted the urge to wipe it on my dress. Jane Bond would not do that, and since I'd already committed to channeling the 007 spy—well, the female version I envisioned in my head—I had to stay in character. As best I could, minus the gun strapped to my thigh because that would be just dangerous; plus I didn't have my gun license, nor concealed weapon permit. Yet. But that was due to change. Tomorrow Captain Cowboy Hotpants—aka Detective Kade Galloway— aka my boyfriend, was taking me out to the shooting range for my first ever lesson. *Lord, help us all.*

"So, this is the museum's annual dinner, huh? Is it always this packed?" I joked.

Anita beamed. She was what I'd call a pleasant woman. Late fifties, silver hair, plumpish figure, and obsessed with the historical society. When she'd called yesterday to request my services, she'd rambled on for some time about her work as president for the society.

From what I could tell, it was mostly event management. In the next month alone, they had planned a tag and bake sale, a movie night, a preservation day open house, and a co-hosted event with the museum—one hundred years of fashion history. Not to mention tonight's little soiree.

"It's an excellent turnout." Anita agreed. "Nearly all the historical society committee is here, along with the museum committee."

"Right, right." I nodded. "So how many are on the historical society committee?"

"Eight."

"And the museum committee?"

"Seven."

Ben snorted. "So they've got, what... five legitimate guests and the rest are all committee members. No wonder they didn't dress up." He turned his attention towards the trestle table. "Man, I wish I could eat food."

"Oh, there's Lacey!" Anita spotted someone across the room and raised her hand to wave. "Please, excuse me for a moment, Audrey. Mingle, get yourself something to eat."

Joining Ben at the buffet, I often wondered what I'd miss the most if I were dead? Coffee! The answer is most definitely coffee. Followed closely by food. Watching the ghost in front of me try to pick up a pinwheel sandwich, I smothered a laugh and followed along behind him, stacking my plate high with treats before finding a vantage point along the far wall where I could study the attendees of tonight's little get-together.

Shoving a ham, cheese, and spinach puff into my mouth, my eyes practically rolled into the back of my head as the flavors burst on my tongue. "Oh, my God. These are amazeballs," I said to no-one in particular, taking another bite before I'd finished the first. Flakes of pastry fluttered down onto my boobs, the pale golden crumbs standing out starkly on my black dress. I shimmied my shoulders to dislodge them, but they were stuck fast.

"Do you really need to look like you're having an orgasm while eating that?" Ben grumbled, drifting over to me. I lifted one shoulder, mindful that we were in a roomful of people, and only I could see him. He pointed to my chest, finger moving around and around in a circular motion. "You've got a little something..."

"I know, I know." Finishing the puff, I blew the remaining crumbs from my fingers and dusted off my boob shelf. This was one reason why I'd worn black. Hides the stains. For invariably, I will spill something on myself. But also, trust me to drop crumbs that stood out starkly against black.

"See anything suspicious?" I said under my breath, eyes scanning the room. People gathered in small groups, huddled together, clutching their paper plates and gossiping up a storm. None of them looked like your typical jewelry thief.

With such a small number of people in such a large room, voices echoed. Someone dropped a pair of serving tongs onto the floor, and the sound bounced harshly around the room. Heads swiveled, and the guilty party blushed and whispered an apology, hurriedly picking up the tongs and placing them back on the table.

"Honestly, Vernon, don't put them back on the table." I recognized Mary Wilson, secretary of the historical society, as she bustled forward, round body waddling side to side as she huffed up to the table and snatched up the serving tongs. "These have been on the floor. I'll get a clean set from the kitchen." Off she went, waddle, waddle, waddle, her arthritic knees refusing to bend. The chatter resumed.

"Why are we here again?" Ben asked, lounging by my side, arms crossed over his chest as he frowned in displeasure at the people in front of us.

"I told you. Anita wanted me to come. She's convinced a member of the committee has stolen her necklace. This was the best way to meet them."

"And why did she think that?"

"Because she mentioned at the last meeting that she would wear the necklace tonight. She only gets it out for special occasions, and tonight is a bit of a big deal for Anita." I picked up an open sandwich from my plate, loaded with what appeared to be chicken, corn, and something red, possibly tomatoes, and shoved it in my mouth. The burst of flavors on my tongue was not what I expected. First up, *not* chicken. Possibly shrimp? Something seafoodish anyway. But the kicker was oh, around three seconds later, when my mouth was on fire.

Schooling my face to hide the inferno happening in my mouth, I rushed to the trestle table, and grabbed a fistful of napkins, turned my back, and spat the partially chewed up sandwich into it. A frantic search for a trash can came up empty, so I stuffed the lot into my purse.

"Everything okay?" Anita Finley reappeared with an attractive redhead in tow. I blinked through watering eyes, opened my mouth to speak, but all that came out was a croak. Oh my lord, I think I'd burned my vocal cords, and I hadn't even swallowed any of the Hellspawn sandwich.

"Ah." The redhead nodded knowingly. "You had one of Eleanor's sandwiches, huh?"

"Mftsh?" I tentatively touched my lips to make sure they were still attached to my face.

"Anita, grab our guest some milk, would you?" The redhead ordered. Anita hurried off to obey. The redhead stood in front of me, blocking me from view of the rest of the room. "Just relax. And breathe. Most of us know to give Eleanor's sandwiches a wide berth.

She just can't seem to grasp the concept of a hint of chili. I don't know exactly how much she puts in her mix, but suffice it to say it's enough to strip the enamel clean off your teeth." Anita came back and shoved a Dixie cup of milk into my hand. I bolted it down, the fire easing somewhat. "What else is in those things?" I gasped. "I thought it was chicken."

"That's her seafood surprise," the redhead replied. "A mixture of crab, shrimp, tomatoes, and cheese."

"And chili," Anita added almost as an apology. "Oh, my gosh!" She suddenly exclaimed. "You're not allergic, are you? I have an EpiPen if you need it. I don't know how many times I've asked Eleanor not to bring seafood dishes—I'm allergic myself—but she continues to ignore me and bring her seafood surprise. We're all so used to it now, and know to avoid it, that it completely slipped my mind to warn you. I'm so sorry."

"It's okay. I'm fine," I said, my mouth now blessedly numb.

"This wouldn't happen if we had the budget for catering," Anita grumbled. "But the books aren't looking so hot this year. We've had to self-cater. Otherwise, I'd get Lacey here to provide the food for all of our events. Oh, how rude. Audrey, this is my best friend, Lacey Stevens. Lacey, this is Audrey Fitzgerald. Lacey is a chef!"

"Is that right?" They had a chef on the committee, and they let things like Eleanor's seafood surprise slip through? But I guess if you didn't have the budget, well, you had to be thankful for potluck dinners.

"Pleased to meet you, Audrey." Lacey Stevens smiled, her auburn curls dancing around her shoulders. I eyeballed her critically. Anita's best friend, huh? She looked to be younger than Anita, in her late forties maybe, with immaculate makeup, rocking a red lip and winged eyeliner not dissimilar to mine, and a chic yellow pantsuit with heels.

"Here, try one of these." Lacey moved with graceful strides to the buffet table and returned, holding a noodle cup on a napkin. "One of my specialties, and something I know Anita can eat." She smiled warmly at her friend. "These are chicken, and the only spices are ginger, garlic, and soy sauce. Oh, and peanut oil. You're not allergic to peanuts, are you?"

"No, thankfully, I'm allergy-free." I cautiously took a bite of the noodle cup, my eyes widening. It was delicious, even my fried taste buds thought so.

"Right?" Anita grinned. "She's the bomb."

"Okay," I said, taking another bite. "I think this just became my favorite dish."

Lacey laughed. "Everyone says that. So, how do you two know each other?"

Anita's face flushed bright red, and panic flitted across her features. Oh boy, I had a sinking feeling she was about to blow my cover. The whole idea of tonight was that I got to meet and question the societies' committee members without them being any the wiser. And definitely not letting them in on the fact that Anita's diamond necklace had been stolen. But all of that had fled Anita's mind, and I knew she was about to spill the beans.

<h1 style="text-align:center">CHAPTER TWO</h1>

"*I* hired Audrey to—" Anita began, but I cut her off.

"Anita hired me to help with the Kelsh estate." I smiled while reaching out to grab Anita's wrist and giving it a hard squeeze. *We talked about this, remember?* I conveyed with my eyes.

"I'm a temp," I explained. "Bit of an expert with spreadsheets and I had a gap in my schedule, so when Anita called to see if I'd be interested in a day or two's work cataloging the estate, well how could I refuse?"

The basis for my cover story was true. I had been an office temp before I was a PI, and Dudley Kelsh had no living heirs, so he'd bequeathed his entire estate to various charities. The contents of his family home went to the historical society. Anita had told me there wasn't anything of value in those contents, just some old furniture and a ton of bric-à-brac, but never-the-less she wanted to see his donation given the proper amount of respect it deserved.

"The Kelsh estate?" Lacey arched one perfectly manicured brow. "I hardly think that requires cataloging. I thought the committee agreed we'd hold a yard sale?"

Anita stiffened. "We did. But we are legally obliged to keep a record of what we're selling or giving away." I had no idea if that were true or not, but I wasn't about to argue the point. Seems Lacey had no such qualms.

"Really, Anita? You're wasting our precious resources on hiring a temp to catalog a lonely old man's junk?" She sniffed. "We'd be better off hiring a skip and cutting our losses."

"Harsh." The word slipped out before I could stop it, and both women looked at me in surprise. I smiled weakly, casting my mind around frantically to cover my outburst when inspiration hit. A good PI needed to think on their feet, and I was starting to believe I had what it took to make a decent career out of this private investigator gig. "When Anita explained the assignment, and that it's on behalf of the society, I immediately waived my fee. So you see, no money wasted. And it's all for a good cause. I'm sure, as a member of the historical society, you'd appreciate that, Lacey?"

Lacey cocked her head and looked me up and

down as if re-evaluating her initial opinion of me. With a slight inclination of her head, she smiled ever so sweetly. "Of course. Would you excuse me for a moment?"

Anita and I watched her walk away. "She's your best friend?" I asked.

"She is," Anita sighed. "I know, I know, everyone thinks we're the odd couple. I mean, look at us. She's beautiful, graceful, stylish. I'm fat, frumpy, and boring." She gave a self-deprecating laugh. "But we just clicked. I've never had a friend like Lacey before. She only moved to Firefly Bay a few months ago to take up the chef position at the hotel. She joined the historical society to make friends, and yeah, here we are. Chalk and cheese."

I gave Anita a reassuring pat on the back. "Friendships come in all shapes and sizes." I looked around the room at the potential suspects. Who here had stolen Anita's necklace? "Right, while we're alone, tell me again what you believe happened to your necklace. And then introduce me to the suspects."

"Right." She nodded. "The committee met last week to discuss this evening's event. Who would open up, who was bringing what dish? I so wish Eleanor had listened and not brought the seafood surprise sandwiches. Again, I'm so sorry."

I waved away her apology. "Who was at the meeting? Everyone? And you mentioned when we spoke before that you'd told them you were planning on wearing your diamond necklace?"

"Yes! Yes, that's why I hired you because I remember specifically telling them I would wear it tonight. I usually keep it tucked away at home, I don't wear it often because I'm so scared of losing it. It was a gift from my parents for my twenty-first birthday. After the meeting, I went home and got it out, I left it sitting on the dresser in my bedroom, in its box. And then yesterday I noticed it was missing. I searched high and low for it, wondering if I'd knocked it to the floor or something, but it was nowhere to be found. That's when I called you."

"And you said some of the committee members were in your house between the night of the meeting and yesterday?"

"Yes." She nodded vigorously. "Not the entire committee mind you. But three of them. And I thought it suspicious, when I looked back on it, that all three had been at the meeting when I mentioned the necklace, and all three had been in my house, and then it goes missing."

"Point out the three." I invited.

"Keagan Dunn popped in." She nodded toward the good-looking art dealer. "He wanted to talk about an old painting we discovered in the attic of the Kelsh estate. Worthless, but pretty enough, and the committee agreed that Keagan could oversee the cleaning and restoration of the piece at his gallery, and then it would be donated to the museum."

Keagan didn't strike me as the type who would swipe a diamond necklace, but I filed away what she'd told me. He was in her house and had the opportunity.

"Who else?"

"Noreen Bellamy." I followed Anita's gaze towards a woman wearing black slacks, a green blouse, with a black waistcoat, the buttons stretching tight across her plump belly. She had shoulder-length reddish-brown hair that lacked any sense of style, and heavy rimmed black glasses. "Noreen is our treasurer," Anita explained. "And she's also my husband Logan's bookkeeper."

"Right." She looked like the bookkeeper type. Either that or librarian. "So she stopped in to talk to you about the society's accounts?"

"No, no. She was there to see Logan. She's been looking after the accounts for his construction business for years. He doesn't share any of that with me. I tried to get involved when he first started the business, but I was a school teacher back then and busy with my own career, and we had Tyler, so I was super busy. Finley Constructions took off, Logan already had an excellent reputation as a builder when he struck out on his own, so it was easier for everyone if he just hired a bookkeeper to take care of things."

"And has that bookkeeper always been Noreen?"

"Good grief, no. Logan started the business twenty-two years ago, he's been through four or five bookkeepers since then. Noreen has been with him for about five years give or take."

Interesting. Would a family friend, one who'd been involved in the financials of Anita's husband's business, be brazen enough to steal from her employer? Or, more precisely, her employer's wife?

"Okay. And who was your third visitor?"

"Mary Wilson, the historical society's secretary. She was dropping off some flyers for the movie night. Each committee member has a commitment to pass around the flyers. Mary designs them, prints them out, and then delivers them to the committee members."

"She delivers them to you?" I was surprised. Mary was not only overweight, but I would have thought her arthritic knees would have been problematic.

Anita grinned. "On her mobility scooter. And a word to the wise, if you see her coming toward you on the sidewalk, get out of her way. She's been known to run over a foot or two."

"Duly noted."

"You know, come to think of it, it couldn't have been Mary," Anita said.

"Oh? Why's that?"

"Well, logistically, I don't think Mary could get up the stairs in my house. Our bedrooms and second bath are upstairs. Living areas downstairs. And the necklace was last seen in my bedroom. Plus, I remember now… she didn't even come inside. She beeped the horn on her scooter, and I came out to collect the flyers from her."

"Right, so we scratch Mary. That leaves Keagan and Noreen."

Anita frowned, and I recognized the look on her face. Remorse. Guilt. She was regretting having me investigate her colleagues, I was sure of it.

"Look." I placed a hand on her shoulder. "You said your son, Tyler, suggested you may have simply lost it? That he remembers saying last time you wore it that the catch was faulty?"

"Finally!" Ben, who'd been spending his time at the buffet table had now rejoined us, threw his hands up in the air. "This has been a wild goose chase not worth your time, Fitz."

"Hush," I scolded him. I was in the middle of soothing Anita, I did not need my ghostly side-kick butting in.

"What was that, dear?" Anita asked, looking at me with a suspicious look on her face, the one that said *you did not just tell me to hush, did you?*

"I said that maybe the necklace is simply lost. Not stolen." I ignored my slip and hoped she would too. I was the only person who could see, hear, and talk to Ben's ghost. And sometimes that was a pain in my butt.

She chewed her lip. "I'd like to think that." Her sigh

was long and heartfelt. "But the problem is, I don't remember taking it out of its box. Or putting it on. So how could I have possibly lost it?"

"It's certainly a conundrum," I agreed. "One that I will get to the bottom of. Let me chat with Keagan and Noreen, and you can get on with enjoying your evening and not worrying about any of this."

"You are such a softie." Ben accused me as we watched Anita Finley join in an animated conversation about highland terriers.

"What do you think happened to the necklace?" I whispered, trying not to move my lips as I spoke.

"Best guess? She knocked it off the dresser. It was still in its box, so I'm guessing she didn't notice it on the floor and has given it a kick and soccered it into some obscure, hard to reach hiding spot. Under the dresser or something."

"She said she searched her room. Thoroughly."

"Have you? Searched for it, I mean. Her idea of a thorough search and your idea of a thorough search are possibly two very different things. Did she move the furniture about?"

"All good points," I sighed. "I'll stop by her house in the morning on my way back from the range and search for it myself."

CHAPTER THREE

Watching Galloway check the clips on the two pistols laid out in front of us had my heart skipping a beat and sweat beading my brow. I'd come into this with a brash confidence that was rapidly retreating the closer I got to holding one of those deadly objects in my hands.

"You need to know how to use this," Galloway said, placing the black pistol he'd been holding back onto the overturned forty-four-gallon drum serving as a counter. "But I hope you never have to."

"So do I…" I couldn't contain the nervous giggle that slipped out. "I'm sorry, it's just… I don't even kill spiders."

"Nor do I. Not with a gun." His joke broke the tension, and I snorted out a laugh. He nodded his head toward the gun. "It's all yours."

When he'd told me we were going to the shooting range, I'd thought he meant the one in town, the one with lanes and barriers and safety equipment. The one where I felt reasonably confident I wouldn't accidentally shoot myself or him. Instead, we were in an abandoned tunnel, part of the old mill that had closed down decades ago, and there were no safety precautions to be seen. Just the tunnel, caved in at the far end, illuminated with two big construction lights, a string with three targets pegged to it, the drum, and us. It had disaster written all over it.

"You come here often?" I asked, wiping my sweaty palms on my jeans.

"Sometimes." He shrugged. "When I need to blow off steam."

"You blow off steam by shooting things?"

"Sometimes. I know you're stalling, Fitz." He shook his head and approached, moving in close behind me. "Safety first," he said, lips close to my ear. I shivered, reached with a trembling hand to pick up the safety glasses and earmuffs. Galloway donned his own gear, then reached over me to pick up the handgun, handing it to me.

"Three things to always remember. One, keep the gun pointed in a safe direction." He gave a nod toward the targets. "Two, keep your finger off the trigger until you're ready to shoot. And keep the gun unloaded until you're ready to use it."

A wave of nausea washed over me. "Got it." Convinced I would puke, I turned to face him, desperate for this to be over with. Guns made me nervous. I really didn't think I had what it took to be a responsible gun owner.

"You've got this, Fitz." Ben, who'd been exploring the old mill, had returned. Startled, I swung toward him, gun raised.

"Whoa!" Galloway grabbed my wrist and swung my arm toward the targets. "That way."

"Right." I nodded, clasped the gun with both hands, screwed my eyes shut and prepared to fire.

"Eyes open," Ben instructed, while Galloway moved in closer, so close I could feel the heat of him along my back and thoughts filtered through my mind, thoughts that had nothing to do with shooting a gun. I was trembling and pretty sure I would pass out or vomit, possibly both.

"Easy." Galloway eased the earmuff away from my ear. "Hold it like this." He positioned my hands correctly, one hand cradling the other. "We'll do two hands to start."

"To start?" I squeaked.

"Mmmm. It may not be possible to always use two hands. You need to be comfortable with a one-hand grip."

I nodded jerkily, my head bumping his. "Take a

breath, raise your arms, level up your target, gently squeeze the trigger."

He released my earmuff, and I did as instructed, swinging my arms up I eyeballed the target, aimed as best I could, and squeezed. The gunshot echoed throughout the tunnel, and the target didn't so much as flutter.

"Not too terrible," Galloway lied, voice raised to be heard through the protective ear wear. "Remember to squeeze the trigger gently, don't jerk it. Try again."

Breathe and squeeze, breathe, and squeeze. Round after round completely missed the target.

"Is this faulty?" I peered at the gun in my hand, twisting it this way and that. How can I not have hit the target yet? Galloway hastily placed his hand over mine and directed the gun back at the target. "Do not shoot yourself. Or me."

"So far, I'm doing a bang-up job of shooting that pile of dirt," I grumbled, my frustration growing. I hadn't expected to be good at this, but I had hoped to at least nick the edge of the target. So far, I had a one hundred percent success rate at missing it altogether.

We stopped to reload, and I paid attention to every movement Galloway made. He'd brought along the Glock and Smith & Wesson that had been in Ben's gun safe. He handed the former to me. "Try this. We'll do one-handed now."

"Right." Why he wanted me to try one-handed when I couldn't hit a non-moving target using both hands was beyond me, but I dutifully faced the target and held my arm straight out in front of me. Galloway maneuvered me until I was side-on, his hands on my shoulders.

"Sideways to the target," he said, brushing my hair away from my neck. "Look along your shoulder, down your arm, straight line to your sights." I did as instructed, trying to ignore the heat curling through me at his nearness.

"Hold it firmly. Legs apart." I was sorely tempted to turn around and plant one on him when his hand flattened against my hip and pressed me against him, my butt snug against his groin.

"Breath in." I sucked in a breath. "Focus." I eyeballed the target lined up in my sights. "Breath out." I released the breath I'd been holding. "Squeeze gently."

I fired, and to my utter surprise, I hit the target. Well, the paper surrounding the target, but at least I hit something this time.

"Great job. Try again, this time on your own." He stepped away, taking his heat with him. I missed it, missed the distraction of him, but more importantly, without that distraction, my focus returned. Standing side on to the target, I shot off round after round, hitting the target twice. Not a bullseye by any means, but I'd hit the outer circle, and I was prepared to take that as a win.

"Well done, Fitz!" Ben shouted, and I smiled weakly. The gun didn't feel natural in my hand like Ben had said it would. He'd promised that once I got used to the weight of it, the feel of it, it would feel right at home. It didn't. It felt like I was visiting Great Aunt Bertha and having high tea using her best china. I didn't have a Great Aunt Bertha, I didn't drink tea, and the thought of handling delicate china was enough to have me breaking out in hives.

I dropped my arm to my side, deflated. "I don't think this is for me." I'd forgotten to take my finger off the trigger and shot a round into the ground next to my foot. I hopped sideways in fright, squeezing the trigger again and shooting off another shot.

"Hey!" Galloway stepped into my personal space and ran his hand down my arm to retrieve the gun. "This is your first go at it. It takes practice."

Pulling my ear muffs down, I squinted at him. "What?"

"I said, great work for your first time."

"I was crap."

"You hit the target." He pointed out. "That's a win."

"I guess?" I wasn't convinced today could be labeled a success. "If the dirt was the target, then I nailed it." Pulling my phone out of my back pocket, I checked the time. "Oh, God. Look at the time. I promised to drop in and see Mrs. Finley."

"Your new client?"

"Yeah. Ben thinks it's a waste of time."

"Oh? Why's that?" Galloway released the clips from both guns and packed them away in the black sports bag from Ben's closet. When Galloway had come downstairs carrying the bag, I'd had a vivid flashback of Ben doing precisely the same thing. It was almost as if an image of Ben was overlaid onto Galloway, and I'd been so overcome, and at a loss for words, I'd simply walked out to the car without a word. Even Ben's scent lingered on the bag, and it was tugging at my heartstrings, months later, that I'd lost my best friend.

"He thinks Mrs. Finley has lost the necklace and that there really isn't a case at all."

"What do you think?" Zipping up the bag, Galloway tossed it over his shoulder and headed out. I followed.

"I'm not sure. She's convinced it was stolen." Ben had accused me of letting my emotions sway my better judgment, that I had too much empathy with Anita Finley.

"Come on, Fitz," Ben whined, walking silently alongside us as we made our way out of the tunnel and into daylight. "You know I'm right. This case is a lost cause. Emphasis on lost."

"Yeah, well, maybe you could do something

helpful, like search her house for it?" I said, waiting while Galloway crossed to a metal box on the outside of the weathered shed that was the entrance to the tunnel and flicked the power switch. "If you'd bothered to come to our initial meeting, you could have found the necklace already, and the case would be solved."

If a ghost could blush, Ben would be blushing right now. As it was, he crossed his arms over his chest and lowered his chin. "I had important business to take care of."

I snorted. "I hardly call watching HSN important business."

"I never thought I'd miss shopping," he sighed. "It's a guilty pleasure that I truly miss."

"What does Ben think of your shooting prowess?" Galloway returned, slinging an arm around my shoulders and dropping a kiss on my cheek, his stubble scraping across my skin and making it tingle.

"Tell him I think a blind monkey would have done better," Ben replied.

"A blind monkey?" I squawked. "I wasn't that bad!" I went to sock him in the shoulder, but being incorporeal, my arm swung through the air and connected with nothing. My forward momentum was too late to stop, and I staggered, nearly knocking myself over. Galloway laughed and held me upright.

"What did he say?" Galloway asked. Now that

Galloway knew I could see and speak with my best friends' ghost, life had been a lot simpler, albeit odd.

"Nothing of any value," I grumbled, composing myself. "But we've gotta go. I'm going to be late."

"I still think this is a waste of time." Ben followed us to the car and seated himself in the back.

"So you keep saying."

"I really think your time would be better spent studying for your exam." He continued on. Honestly, on the nagging scale, Ben was worse than my mom.

"Don't remind me." I turned and eyeballed him over the back of the seat. "I mean it, Ben. Don't remind me. I know my PI exam is coming up, I don't need you in my ear about it twenty-four-seven." My stomach was in knots as it was.

Galloway patted my knee. "You will be fine. You'll ace it." One of the many things I liked about Kade Galloway was not only how tolerant he was at having a ghost as a third wheel, but how he had the uncanny knack of following our conversations. Given that he only heard one side of it, it was quite a skill.

"Tell me more about this case. Why doesn't Ben approve?"

I filled him in on the missing diamond necklace and how Ben thought it was simply lost, not stolen. By the time we arrived home, I'd finished the story and could tell by Galloway's face that he was leaning towards Ben's take on the situation. He opened his mouth to speak, but I held up my hand to stop him. "It doesn't matter what you think. I took the case. It's my case. Not Ben's. Not yours. If I eventually come to the same conclusions the two of you have jumped to, then I will tell Mrs. Finley myself."

"Okay, okay. Point taken." Then he kissed me, and any disquiet that had been rattling around inside my head vanished in an instant. This man could kiss. Winding my arms around his neck and ignoring the dig of the gear stick in my ribs, I practically purred.

"Ahem?" Ben's face appeared frightfully close, and I reared back with a squeak.

"Don't do that!" I gasped, hand to my chest.

"Ben, my man," Galloway drawled in that rumbly, sexy voice of his. "Do we need to have a talk? No interrupting when we're having... adult time."

Ben laughed and walked through the front of the car. "No, no, we're good."

Through gritted teeth, I translated, adding, "he's walking through the car. He knows I hate that. He's being a dick."

"I heard that!" Ben called from outside. "But if you don't stop sucking face, you will be late."

Darn him for being right. "He's right. I will be late. I gotta run. We still on for lunch?"

"Absolutely. Call me when you're finished with your client."

A quick peck goodbye, and I hopped out of

Galloway's car and hurried to my own. My brand-new Honda CR-V was tucked up in the garage, and while I mourned Ben's Nissan Rogue that I accidentally totaled, I was one hundred percent in love with my new ride. It was a gorgeous metallic blue, came with a push-button start and reversing cameras. It was, in short, perfection.

Connecting my phone to the car's entertainment system through the Bluetooth, I called Mom as I made my way to Anita's house to discuss my findings from last night's dinner. We'd agreed to meet at ten, and I had a little under five minutes if I wanted to be on time.

"Audrey, love, how are you?"

"Hey, Mom." I took the corner a little fast in my hurry to get to Anita's, and the tires screeched on the asphalt. I eased off the accelerator. Me and fast cars were not a good combination.

"What was that?" Mom asked. "Are you driving?"

"It's fine, Mom. Hands free."

"Audrey..." I heard the stress and worry in her voice, and I couldn't blame her. I was always doing something to send her blood pressure through the roof.

"Honestly, Mom, everything is fine. Look, quick call 'cos I'm on my way to meet a client, can I get your chicken pot pie recipe?"

"Audrey Fitzgerald, are you planning on cooking?"

"Har har, Mom. Can you just email it to me? Please?"

"Planning a special meal for Kade?" She pressed, and I rolled my eyes. Yes, I was officially dating Captain Cowboy Hot Pants, Kade Galloway, the hottest detective in Firefly Bay. I could hardly believe it myself. Not the hot part, that was no contest. The cop part. Ever since Ben had been forced out of the force, I'd held a grudge against cops. They were dirty, and I didn't trust them. But Galloway had managed to get under my defenses and convince me not all cops were bad. It helped that he was heading up a secret investigation into corruption within the Firefly Bay Police Department.

"I thought it was time." I sighed. "He needs to know what he's in for."

Ben, who was riding shotgun next to me and had remained blissfully silent until now, snorted. "Got that right. Better get the poor guy some Alka Seltzer."

"Okay, darling, I'll send it through. When's the big date?" Mom said.

"I haven't decided yet. We're meeting for lunch, so I'll see what his shifts are like in the next week."

"Oh good, you can schedule in our family dinner with him as well. Don't you think it's time we all met him?"

"Mom," I whined, "y'all know the man already. It's not like he's a stranger."

She sniffed. "Well, yes, we know him to say hello to in the street, but we don't know, know him."

"I'm not sure he's ready for our family yet." I protested.

"Nonsense. Bring him tomorrow night. I insist."

"We'll see. I'm not making any promises. Okay, gotta go, Mom. See ya." I disconnected the call before she could get another word in.

Pulling up at the curb outside of Anita's house, I killed the engine. "You're going to take Kade to family dinner?" Ben asked, eyebrows raised.

"Ludicrous idea, right?"

"He's got to meet them sometime." Ben pointed out.

"Does he, though?" I climbed out of the car and slammed the door, hurrying down the front path of Anita's house and ringing the doorbell. Within seconds the door was flung open, and Anita's son, Tyler, stood looking at me, face initially filled with a warm smile of welcome that quickly slid into disappointment.

"Not who you were expecting?" I asked. Tyler Finley was a blond, blue-eyed, teenage dream. At twenty, he was a very handsome young man, and I imagined he'd set many a young girl's hearts to fluttering. I cocked my head, admiring the way he made blue jeans and a white t-shirt look like it was straight out of the pages of a fashion magazine.

"If you're looking for mom, she's not here." He

looked over my head as if hoping to see someone else behind me.

"Oh? Darn, I thought she said to meet here this morning... maybe she meant the historical society?"

"Probably." Tyler shrugged. "She wasn't meant to be the clean-up crew, but you know Mom, always sticking her nose in. Doesn't trust them to do the job properly." He shut the door in my face, and I stepped back in surprise.

"Okay," I said under my breath, spinning on my heel and heading back to my car. Now I would be late because I'd turned up at the wrong meeting place.

"I could have sworn she said to meet at her house at ten."

"Maybe something happened?" Ben suggested. "Maybe one of the cleanup crew didn't turn up, and she had to step in?"

"Possibly." I fired up the engine, checked my mirrors, and pulled out. "Only one way to find out."

Last night had been a bust regarding the case. I'd chatted with Keagan and Noreen and hadn't been able to glean anything useful from either of them. Just in case any of the other committee members could shed light on the missing necklace, I'd spent time with them too. Nothing. Nothing of interest anyway. Lots of gardening tips and multiple invitations to join the historical society, though.

CHAPTER FOUR

There were two cars in the parking lot of the historical society slash museum, and neither of them was Anita's. Never-the-less I pulled in next to them and went inside, wouldn't hurt to check to see if anyone had seen her.

"Oh, hey, Audrey, come to lend a hand?" Keagan Dunn approached with a garbage bag in hand and a twinkle in his eye.

"Nope. I'm looking for Anita. Is she here?"

"Haven't seen her." Noreen Bellamy called out as she walked past carrying a fold-up chair. "She may have been here earlier, though. Have you checked her office?"

"She has an office?"

Keagan dropped the bag and stripped off his gloves. "Here, I'll show you. She's often here on weekends. Poor love, I don't think she has much of a home life if you know what I mean?"

I followed Keagan from the modern glass structure of the museum to the rustic stone bricks of the historical society. The main door, a heavy wooden affair, was closed, and when he tried the handle, locked. Reaching into his pocket, he produced a set of keys. Noticing me watching, he said, "we all have a set."

"All?" That was a lot of keys to have kicking around.

"Well, not the entire committee, obviously. But those holding official positions. The president, vice-president, treasurer, and secretary."

"Right." I nodded, following him inside. It was dim and cold on the other side of the door, and I shivered, rubbing my hands up and down my arms for warmth.

The building was old but beautiful. A staircase led to the second floor, the green floral carpet and worn banister revealing its age.

"Okay." Keagan stopped. "You know this building was the old firehouse, right?"

I nodded. "I do." The bell tower on the roof was a giveaway.

"This side of the building was the dorm rooms for the firemen on duty. And this side—" he pointed in the other direction, "is where they housed the equipment. Of course, the building has been renovated quite a bit since then, but we've managed to keep a hold of a lot of its original charm, I think."

"It's lovely." I agreed. But it was cold. And it smelled old. Musty. My nose twitched.

"We hold the public functions in the old garage area, makes one nice sizeable room you see. And then there are offices, the kitchen and bathroom, and some smaller meeting rooms if required in the old dorm area." He began walking, and I followed. "Anita's office is just down here to the left."

"What's upstairs?" I asked.

"Mostly storage. It's awkward up there, the roof trusses don't allow for much space. We think it was mostly an access point to get to the bell tower."

He stopped in front of a closed-door then rapped his knuckles on it. "Don't think she's here," he said. He twisted the knob just to be sure, his face revealing his surprise when it turned, and the door swung open.

"She usually keeps that locked, I assume?" I stepped past him and into Anita's office. It was a squeeze. There was barely room for a desk and a filing cabinet.

"She does." Keagan nodded. "Well, suffice it to say she's not here. You can leave her a message if you like?" He indicated the post-it notes lying on her desk.

"That's okay. I'll call her. We had a meeting this morning at ten, only I thought it was at her house, but she's not there either. I thought maybe she was here."

"She usually is. Like I said, she doesn't have much of a home life. I overheard her and Lacey talking.

Apparently, Logan is having an affair." He leaned in conspiratorially, eager to pass on the gossip.

"Really?" She hadn't mentioned it to me, and I would have thought if you'd hire a private investigator to find a missing necklace, why wouldn't you hire them to confirm your husband was cheating on you? "Do you think he is?"

Keagan shrugged. "I will say I was surprised, I mean, an affair? How cliché."

"So you don't think he's having an affair?" Make up your mind, man.

He chuckled. "Look, all I know is that Logan hasn't been his usual self. I'm not convinced of the affair angle myself, but Lacey swears that must be it. Anita will only agree to the fact that he's definitely keeping something from her." He glanced at his watch. "I've got to get back and help Noreen finish cleaning up. Don't know where Lacey got to, she's rostered on as well, she should be here."

I stepped out of Anita's office and waited while Keagan closed and locked her door. "So, there's usually three of you on clean-up duty?"

"Yeah. Only takes about an hour with three of us. Everyone takes leftovers home on the night, so we don't have to deal with food. It's more taking out the trash, packing up the trestle table and the chairs, and then giving the floor a good sweep — and a mop if it needs it."

"Okay. Well, thank you for checking for me." I preceded him down the hallway and out the main entrance, waiting once more while he locked up.

"Actually, she might be out at the Kelsh estate," he said, pocketing the keys and turning to face me, brows drawn low, eyes narrowed. "Isn't that what your meeting is about? The Kelsh estate? I heard last night that Anita had hired you to catalog the contents?"

"I'm volunteering." It was the cover story we'd come up with, and it seems word had got around fast. "I have a couple of days to spare between assignments, and spreadsheets are my thing."

"We couldn't convince you to join the historical society permanently?"

"Sorry, no. But I'm happy to help on this occasion." And I realized that I may just have to follow through and catalog the contents of the Kelsh estate for real. "Do you have the address?" I smiled. "I may as well check if Anita's there. And you're right, maybe she meant to meet me there all along." Though it was odd she hadn't told me that, nor given me the address.

"Sure. What's your number, I'll text it to you?" After exchanging numbers, my phone beeped, and the text message with Dudley Kelsh's address appeared on my screen.

"Thanks, Keagan, I'll leave you to it."

"Anytime. Don't be a stranger."

I returned to my car, glancing around for a sign of

Ben. I hadn't seen him since we'd arrived and assumed he'd gone off to explore, but I couldn't very well call out to him. "Darn it, where are you?" I whispered, climbing into my car and punching Dudley Kelsh's address into the GPS. Then a movement caught my eye, up in the bell tower. Leaning forward, I peered through the windshield, and there was Ben, valiantly trying to ring the bell. I smothered a laugh as I watched him reach for, and disappear through, the bell time after time. I wondered if I should tell him the mechanism had been removed years ago?

Shaking my head, I started the car, braced myself, and sure enough, he was in the passenger seat a second later. "Having fun?" I teased.

"I've been doing research."

"Oh?" Reversing out of my parking spot, I turned onto Summer Street. The Kelsh estate was on the outskirts of town, a twenty-minute drive tops.

"Yeah. That some spirits can touch and move objects."

I glanced at him as he tried to lay his hand on the dash, only it sank right through. "Where have you been doing this research?"

"Documentaries. Sometimes I go to the library and check out what the kids are reading, read over their shoulder if it's anything paranormal."

"Ewww. Creepy."

"They don't know I'm there. And it's not like I can

check out a book myself. Not that they do that much anymore, anyway. So much of it is electronic." His pout was real, his bottom lip poking out a good inch.

"So? What did you discover?" My question distracted him out of his sulk.

"Pay dirt!" He grinned. "There's this kid, Alys, and she's researching the paranormal for a class project, and she's studying—"

"Don't tell me, ghosts." Rolling to a halt at the end of Summer Street, I checked the GPS and flicked my indicator to turn left onto Sunshine Avenue. Whoever named these streets must have been a massive fan of summer, I thought to myself, half-listening to Ben, half concentrating on where I was going, all the while pondering what Keagan had said about Anita and her husband, Logan. Was her husband's supposed affair what this was really about? Was the missing necklace a ruse? But she hadn't even hinted at there being another reason why she'd hired me. She'd had me attend last night's dinner to meet and question the committee members, her husband hadn't even been in attendance.

Spousal investigation was one of the prime reasons a person hired a PI. My PI course had all the statistics, and I knew most of my cases would be proving someone was having an affair or proving they weren't. In the end, it all boiled down to secrets. Who was keeping them, and why?

The drive out to the Kelsh estate gave me time to gather my thoughts to a certain degree. To be honest, I wasn't any closer to finding out who had stolen Anita's necklace, and why. If it even was stolen. Jewelry theft usually stemmed from greed—steal the jewelry, sell it, pocket the proceeds. Yet Anita's necklace wasn't worth much at all. Under a hundred dollars. The diamond itself was of poor quality, the chain was nine carats. Who in their right mind would steal it? I hated to admit it, but Ben just might be right.

Turning off the highway onto a dirt track, I slowed to a crawl as I navigated the potholes. "Is the Kelsh estate a farm?" Ben asked, gazing out the window at the fields surrounding us.

"It's looking that way." We bounced through a pothole, the car violently twisting one way, then the other, jarring my bones.

"Easy, Fitz." Ben tried to clutch the armrests, and I saw his foot pumping for the brake.

"Relax. It's fine." But I eased my foot off the accelerator some more. "If we go much slower, we'll be stationary."

"Maybe I'll go on ahead," Ben said through clenched teeth.

"You're really giving me a complex about my driving," I complained, giving him the side-eye.

"You totaled my car!"

"It was an accident!"

Before we could get into another argument about my driving, we rounded the corner, and a house came into view. For some reason, the Kelsh estate sounded fancy in my head. Like... mansion-esque. What lay before me was anything but. A beaten-up old farmhouse, a weatherboard structure on a distinct lean, gutters hanging off, what was once a picket fence now only had a few sections still standing. And amongst it all, junk. Bicycles, wheelbarrows, a bathtub! There was a rusted car body in the front garden, overgrown with grass and weeds. Nearby was an old barn that looked to be in similar, if not worse, shape.

"This was not what I was expecting," I said, mouth agape. No wonder Lacey had suggested a skip. The whole place looked like it needed to be bulldozed.

"Look!" Ben said, "is that Anita's car?"

A baby blue hatchback was parked at the side of the house. "Yes, it is." I pulled up behind it.

"I think I can see her inside." Ben pointed toward the side window, and I peered through the grimy glass, just making out a silhouette moving backward and forwards. Climbing out of the car, I picked my way around rubble, weeds, and debris to the front door, calling out as I went, "Anita? It's me, Audrey. I'm so sorry I'm late, I thought we were meant to meet at your house, it's taken a bit of time for me to track you down."

"Audrey, thank goodness!" Anita called back. "I'm having trouble with the door."

"Oh? Is it stuck?" I wrapped my fingers around the doorknob and turned. It was stiff but not stuck. Pushing the door open, I stepped inside. Anita had been busy. The front room was mostly cleared out, just an old sofa and coffee table remained, and a bunch of cardboard boxes stacked against one wall.

"Eeew. What's that smell?" I waved my hand in front of my nose. Whatever it was, it was gross.

"That'd be the kitchen." Anita appeared in the doorway, wringing her hands. "Dudley wasn't much on cleaning. Or throwing out the trash."

"Everything okay?" She looked stressed and pale.

"Oh, yes, everything is fine. I just couldn't get the door open, and I think I panicked."

"Ummm. Audrey?" Ben, who'd stayed outside to check out the rusted car, now stepped through the door.

"Oh, my!" Anita gasped, hand to her chest. "Who's this?"

"What?" I looked from Ben to Anita and back again. "You can see him?"

"Of course, I can see him. He's standing right there!" She pointed at Ben, who looked at me. My mouth dropped open. If she could see Ben, that meant that she could either see ghosts too or...

"I think she's dead," Ben mouthed at me. I had a

sinking feeling he was right. She had the same pale appearance Ben had. Washed out. No longer living, breathing, vibrant color.

"How long have you been here, Anita?" I asked, crossing to her side, reaching out an arm to wrap around her shoulders, only that familiar icy prickle bathed my skin where we touched. I dropped my arm. She was incorporeal.

"Errr." She chewed her lip. "I'm a bit fuzzy today, to be honest."

"That's okay." I soothed. "We'll work it out." Anita Finley was dead and didn't know it. I stepped around her and peered into the kitchen, covering my nose and mouth with my elbow against the stench. The rubbish was ankle-deep, and I thought I saw a rodent dart across a filthy countertop. Thankfully, Anita's body was not in the kitchen, so I reached in and tugged the door closed, hoping to lock most of the foul smell in.

"What are you working on?" I asked, heading further into the house.

"Oh, I've been up in the attic." She followed me. "We found that painting up there, the one Keagan is restoring, and I wondered if there was anything else salvageable up there. I hate to admit it, but I think Lacey was right. We're better off hiring a rubbish removal firm."

I approached the retractable ladder in the hallway. "Tell me about the painting." I was hoping to distract her, my heart rate picking up a notch as I climbed the ladder to the attic, bracing myself to the fact that I was most likely about to find Anita's body.

"It was just leaning up against a wall up here, covered in dust and cobwebs. It was of a lady playing the piano. Another lady was singing, and a man was sitting watching them both."

"Odd that it was up in the attic and not hanging on a wall," I muttered, heaving myself up the last rung. There was a battery-operated lamp standing on the floor next to the body of Anita Finley.

"Damn," I whispered, then over my shoulder, "Ben!"

"On it." He appeared by my side in an instant.

"Oh, my goodness!" Anita cried. "Who's that, what's happened?" She rushed forward, then skidded to a halt, hands to her mouth, eyes round with horror.

"Anita, I'm so sorry. There's no easy way to say this. I'm afraid you're dead." I grimaced and shot a look to Ben, who had been examining Anita's body but now straightened and crossed to her ghost.

"We haven't been properly introduced," he said, placing a comforting arm around her shoulders and turning her away from the corpse on the floor. "My name is Ben Delaney, and I'm a ghost."

As Ben led her away, filling her in on his existence in the spiritual world, I knelt by her body. Her face was swollen, the skin flushed, blotchy and red. One arm was thrown out to the side and a few inches from her fingers a half-eaten noodle cup. Nearby sat a plastic container with the lid sealed. Picking it up, I pried open one corner and peeked inside. More noodle cups.

"Anita, were these left-overs from last night?" I called. At least Anita hadn't reacted like the last ghost client. There was no screaming, wailing, or tears from Anita Finley.

"Yes. The chicken noodle cups Lacey made." She crossed back to me, stood dispassionately over her own body, and tapped her chin with a finger. "I think I had an allergic reaction," she said, pointing at her face. "That swelling, and the blotchy skin? Typical signs. But why didn't I get my EpiPen out? I would have felt the reaction coming on, there's enough time to stop it."

"Where would your EpiPen be?" Ben asked.

She pointed to her purse. "In there. I always have it with me. Always. Although I wonder what triggered it? I know there's no seafood in Lacey's noodle cups."

Lifting the container, I took a sniff. Ben and Anita watched me expectantly. "Nope, I can't smell any seafood," I told them. "I wonder if you developed another allergy? Something new? Something different? A mold spore or dust mite or something? This place is teeming with pathogens, and if you're sensitive to that type of thing, it wouldn't be a stretch that you could develop an unexpected allergic reaction."

"Yes. You could be right." Anita crossed her arms

over her chest. "The air in this house was making me cough." Then she turned her attention to Ben. "Is this why I couldn't open the door?"

He nodded. "Yep. Good news and bad news. The bad news is you can no longer touch things. Your hand will pass right through. Good news is, most of the time, you don't need to. Want to open a door? Just walk right through." He demonstrated by walking through the wall of the house to stand in midair outside the cracked attic window.

"Ben," I warned. Him doing that sort of thing freaked me out. He grinned and stepped back inside. "Audrey doesn't like me hovering in the air. Or walking around in her car."

"How come she can see you? Us?" Anita asked.

"Good question," Ben replied. "We think it was something to do with when I died. A woman practicing witchcraft tried to save me, and she was partway through the spell when I passed."

"In that case, why can't everyone see you?"

"Because I was thinking about Audrey at the time I died. And somehow, my spirit became attached to her."

"Oh! Are you two...?"

"No, we're just friends. It took me a while to recall the actual dying part. But I remember a thought crossing my mind that Fitz would be mad as hell at me for dying. And then my cat, Thor, turned up, and both he and Audrey were my last conscious thought when I took my final breath."

My eyes misted at the memory. Despite having ghost Ben, I still mourned the death of my friend and hearing him recount it now caused a lump in my throat. Desperate for a distraction, I picked up Anita's bag and rummaged inside. She said she kept an EpiPen with her at all times, yet I couldn't see one in her bag.

"Anita? You sure your EpiPen was in here? You didn't switch it to an evening purse or something for last night's dinner?"

"No," she snorted. "I'm not that fancy. I only have one purse. That one." She pointed to the navy-blue tote I was holding. "It has to be in there."

"Must be buried at the bottom." I crawled a few feet away and upended the contents of the bag onto the floor. Out clattered an e-reader, phone, purse, lip balm —several, a hairbrush, tissues, a diary organizer that was bulging at the seams, a notebook, nearly a dozen pens, reading glasses and sunglasses. But no EpiPen.

"Maybe she's lying on it?" Ben suggested. "Like she said, she'd have recognized the signs and would have attempted to give herself the shot."

"True." I crawled back to Anita's body, placed a hand against her hip and one against her shoulder, and attempted to roll her, but of course, she was a dead weight. "Urgh," I grunted. "Harder than it looks."

"Does it really matter?" Anita asked. "Either way, I'm still dead."

"True," I replied, still trying to roll her enough to see if she was lying on the EpiPen. "But, we have to rule out foul play."

"Foul play?" Her voice rose. "You suspect foul play?"

"Not necessarily," Ben reassured her. "But any unexpected death should be investigated."

"Right. Yes. Of course." Her head was nodding up and down in understanding, but her hands were busy clasping and unclasping, revealing her agitation. I glanced at Ben. "Maybe you should wait outside?" I suggested. "I'm going to call the police, and then I'll join you."

"Good idea."

I waited until they'd both silently descended the ladder, lips twitching that they went through the motions for my benefit, then returned to my attempts of moving Anita's body. I'd worked out if I rolled her toward me, rather than trying to push her away, I could move her. And despite that victory, still no EpiPen.

CHAPTER FIVE

fter putting in a call to the Firefly Bay Police Department, I followed my instincts. And my instincts told me Anita Finley was murdered. My best guess? The noodle cups were contaminated with seafood, and the perpetrator had stolen her EpiPen. With my spidey senses tingling, I hurried downstairs. I remembered seeing a pair of rubber gloves on the coffee table in the living room. I only had a few minutes to go through Anita's belongings before the police arrived and took everything into evidence. That's if they even treated her death as murder.

Donning the gloves, I scrambled back up the attic ladder and made my way to the contents of Anita's bag. Opening the diary planner, I flicked through the pages. There was an entry for last night's dinner, another this morning that said Kelsh. No mention of our meeting. I snapped a photo of the week's entries, then turned my attention to the notebook. It appeared to be notes on the Kelsh estate, a rough catalog of Anita's findings.

"Interesting..." I lifted the notebook to the light, peering at the spiral binding. A page had been torn out, the tattered stubs caught in the wire. I painstakingly photographed each page and had just set the notebook down when I heard sirens in the distance. I hurriedly took photos of the attic, Anita's body, anything, and everything was memorialized on my phone. I'd sift through it all later. Finally, I broke off a piece of the noodle cup resting in her palm and wrapped it in a tissue.

Hurrying down the ladder, I tossed the gloves back on the coffee table and slid my phone into my back pocket before opening the front door and crossing to my car, casually placing the wadded up tissue with the remnants of noodle cup into the glove box before returning to the porch to wait for the police car that was making its way down the rough track. The siren had been killed, but the lights still flashed, strobing in red and blue against the house as it came to a stop behind mine and Anita's cars. Behind the wheel, Sergeant Dwight Clements, in the passenger seat, Officer Ian Mills.

I bit my tongue to keep from groaning. As far as I was concerned, they were two of the most incompetent members of the Firefly Bay police force. Mills especially has made my life miserable, having taken an apparent dislike to me. He'd taken to pulling me over for fake infringements. I was convinced he'd intentionally busted out my tail light just so he could book me for it. But Galloway had assured me he was on top of it, that his secret investigation into Mills and Clements, plus others, was well underway. It wouldn't be long before his case would blow the corruption wide open and we'd be rid of the bad apples. It couldn't happen soon enough.

Ben, having seen who'd turned up, joined me on the porch. "Call Galloway. Before they do anything stupid."

"What? Like, arrest me?" I whispered. It wouldn't be the first time. I pulled out my phone and called Galloway, hating that I needed this level of protection.

"Finished with your client already?" Galloway answered on the first ring.

"Hold on a second," I replied, then lowered the phone, keeping the call open so he could listen in.

"Officers, her body is upstairs, in the attic." I moved aside as they approached, the steps up to the porch creaking in protest at their combined weight.

Mills looked me up and down, a sneer curling his lip. "Always sticking your nose in where it's not wanted."

"Hardly." I shot back. "Anita Fielding was my client, I had a meeting scheduled with her."

"So just a coincidence that wherever you are, a dead body turns up?" Clements snapped, eyes flashing.

"No such thing as a coincidence," Mills said, brushing past me and giving me a hard nudge with his elbow, making me stagger.

"Asshole." Ben hissed, clenching his fists. I wanted to reassure him it was okay, that I expected nothing less, but I couldn't risk talking to him in front of these two.

"Stay here and don't move." Clements pointed at me and then the porch. "Do not move from this spot. I mean it." His hand rested on the revolver attached to his belt.

"I've no intention of going anywhere, officer. Steer clear of the kitchen, though. There's a reason the door's closed."

He sniffed and headed inside without replying, Mills close behind. Lifting the phone back up to my ear, I said, "get that?"

"I did," Galloway replied. "Where are you?"

"Dudley Kelsh's house. I'll send you the address."

"On my way. Stay away from those two, okay?"

"You don't have to tell me twice." After disconnecting the call, I forwarded on the text I'd received from Keagan that had Dudley's address, then turned to Ben and Anita.

"While we wait, let's go through your morning," I suggested, keeping my voice low and the phone to my ear in case I was overheard talking to myself. "I thought we were meant to meet this morning at ten, but when I got to your place, you weren't home." I directed my statement to Anita. She clamped a hand over her mouth in horror. "Oh, my gosh! You're right! I'm so sorry, I admit, it totally slipped my mind that we had a meeting."

I nodded, I figured as much. "I'm not one for gossip, but given the circumstances, I think this is important..." I began.

"Oh?"

"Keagan mentioned something to me this morning. He said you thought your husband was having an affair—" I ignored her startled gasp and continued, "was that why you were distracted this morning? Did something happen at home?"

"Why would he even say that?" She protested, running her hands over her stomach and looking downright flustered.

"Apparently, he heard it from Lacey."

She blinked in surprise. "Lacey?"

I nodded. "Yep. So is there anything you wanted to tell me?" I paused, waiting for her to blurt out the truth, but she remained stubbornly silent. "I'm not asking to be nosy or to gossip." I pointed out. "But things have changed, Anita. You're dead."

"I never thought he was having an affair." She said. "It was Lacey who kept bringing that up."

"Oh?"

"I told her he wasn't himself. That something was troubling him, and when I asked him about it, he said everything was fine. But I knew that it wasn't. I was concerned he didn't feel he could tell me what was bothering him, but I never thought he was having an affair." An edge of annoyance colored her words.

"But Lacey did, obviously," Ben said.

Anita rolled her eyes. "All that woman thinks about is sex, honestly. She's my best friend, and I love her, but good lord, she has a one-track mind. Every time I mentioned my problems with Logan, she brought up the affair thing. Whenever she came around, and Tyler was home, she'd tease him about having a girlfriend."

"Does he? Have a girlfriend?" I asked out of curiosity. I'd be surprised if he didn't, being such an attractive young man. He'd acted disappointed when he opened the door and saw it was me on the doorstep like he'd been waiting on someone else.

"He's started seeing someone but won't tell me who," Anita admitted. "He's as secretive as his father."

The front door suddenly smashed open, and Mills barreled through, hand over his mouth, his face an interesting shade of green. Bolting down the front steps, he vomited all over what was once a garden bed but was now a jumble of weeds.

"Gross," Ben said, crossing his arms over his chest and watching the overweight man retch repeatedly until there was nothing left to bring up. Wiping his mouth on the back of his sleeve, Mills straightened.

"Found the kitchen then?" I asked poker-faced. "I warned you not to go in there." He scowled but didn't say a word, stomping back inside, mouth, and nose burrowed in the crook of his elbow. With the front door standing open, the stench from the kitchen wafted out.

"Let's go stand over there." I pointed to the rear of the patrol car. "You guys can't smell, but I can, and those two have disturbed something putrid in the kitchen, I can smell it from here."

"It's funny how you get used to it," Anita said, following me. "The first time I stepped inside this house, I nearly passed out from the smell. But then I just acclimatized, I guess."

"I wonder if that's it?" Ben said. "Seafood in the kitchen. Particles of it in the air, and you breathed it in, and it triggered your allergy."

I frowned. "I've never heard of that before. Do you think it's possible?"

"Doubtful," Anita said. "I've been in fish markets before, and the smell hasn't triggered an allergic reaction. I have to ingest it."

"There goes that theory." Ben shrugged.

"Plus, if that were true, she'd have used her EpiPen. Only I couldn't find it. I searched your bag, under your body... it's nowhere to be found."

Anita frowned. "That can't be right. I always carry it with me. That's why I only use the one handbag, so I don't forget to switch it over."

"How sensitive is your allergy?" Ben asked.

"Very. Just a morsel of any seafood is enough to send me into anaphylaxis."

"Fish and crustaceans?"

She nodded. "And mollusks. Some people aren't allergic to all three, they can eat some seafood, but I drew the short straw. I have to watch out for sauces and salad dressing too."

"Really? There's seafood in sauce?" Ben asked.

"There is. Besides the obvious oyster sauce and fish sauce, there's anchovies in Worcestershire sauce and some brands of soy sauce, so it's not as simple as avoiding fish on the menu, it can pop up anywhere—which is why I always have my EpiPen with me. There is absolutely, categorically, no way I would not have it with me."

I looked at Ben, who looked back at me, face solemn. I knew I was right, knew that Anita had been murdered, but glancing back at the house, I doubted very much that Sergeant Clements and Officer Mills would reach the same conclusion.

"Have you had to use it recently?" I asked. "No chance you used it and forgot to get a new one? They're a one time use, right?"

"They are single-use, yes, but you get two per pack,

and I still have one in the box at home. Once I've used the one I carry with me, I'll get a prescription for another pack, so I'm never in the situation of not having an EpiPen at my disposal."

Ben turned to me. "Sounds like she's all over it. Highly doubtful she wouldn't take her EpiPen with her, especially knowing she has a deadly allergy."

"Wait." Anita stepped closer. "You're saying someone did this intentionally? You think I was murdered?" She'd been remarkably cool, calm, and collected up until this point, surprisingly accepting of her recent demise. "But who would murder me?" The last was said in a sob, and I shot a look at Ben. I couldn't comfort her, she was incorporeal, and I didn't fancy shoving my hand through a ghost thank you very much. He pulled Anita into a hug, tucking her head beneath his chin. Where their ghostly bodies collided, little sparkles danced in the air.

I moved away, giving them space while Ben muttered soothing words to the dead woman. Inside I could hear the house creak and groan as the two policemen moved around. I wondered if overweight Mills would go through a rotten floorboard, and my lips curled at the visual forming in my brain. Then I heard a curse and thundering footsteps, could visually track the noise through the house until Mills stormed out, heading straight for me. I instinctively backed up a few steps, but then made myself stop and hold my ground.

"You!" He snarled, face red with anger, finger poking me in the chest. "Are a pain in my ass."

"I aim to please." I shot back, refusing to be intimidated.

"I just got a call from your boyfriend. Detective Galloway. Why did you have to go and call him, huh? Now he's all up in my grill that some broad has kicked it in this dump."

"It was a personal call," I replied. "We had a date. Obviously, I'm going to be late." I waved an arm vaguely in the direction of the house. Ben and Anita had fallen silent, no doubting watching Officer Mills approaching explosion point. I cocked my head, wondering if his head would actually pop off. His eyes were bulging, his skin so red it was as if he had a nasty sunburn. I didn't need to look to know his hands would be clenched into fists.

He leaned over me, so close his belly pushed me, and I almost took a step back to get away from the unpleasant aroma of his body odor, not to mention breath, as he barked into my face, "I've had it up to here with you, you interfering bi—"

"Language, Officer Mills." I cut him off. "That's no way to speak to a member of the public."

"Hey!" Ben shouted, crossing to us. "Get away from her, you jerk." I felt the icy rush as Ben made a lunge for Mills and passed right through. I shot him a look. *You can't help me.*

Mills stubby fingers gripped the fabric of my T-shirt, pulling the collar tight in his fist, and jerking. I felt the fabric rip. "I'm warning you, Fitzgerald," his voice dropped, low and menacing, and a shiver danced up my spine. I'd never particularly thought of Mills as a physical threat before, just a moron who hides behind the power of his badge, but now I was rethinking things. We were out on the Kelsh farm. Isolated. Anything could happen. Bad things could happen. I was pretty sure it was Mills who'd broken into my apartment, the one who hip and shouldered me over the railing in his bid to escape a few short weeks ago, but I had no proof.

"Let. Her. Go!" Ben was wildly throwing punches and was so comical my lips twitched. Big mistake. Mills naturally assumed my mirth was directed at him and not the ghost valiantly trying to pulverize him with incorporeal fists. His temper exploded. Grabbing my shirt with both hands, he lifted me off my feet, shaking me in anger. I was so surprised I dangled like a rag doll, momentarily stunned.

"Oh, my!" Anita gasped. Ben went ballistic. "Use your knees, Fitz," he shouted. "That old Fitzgerald ball buster should do the trick."

Ah yes, I'd brought many a man to his knees with a knee to his groin. Only I was at the wrong angle and had nothing to brace myself on since my feet were currently several inches off the ground. Which left me one course of action. Take back my power. Wrapping my legs as best as I could around the plump man's waist, I anchored myself to him, leaned back to get some momentum, then shot forward, slamming my forehead into his.

The headbutt was effective. Mills released me with a yowl, staggering backward with both hands to his forehead. I didn't have enough time to get my legs beneath me. I crashed backward, my butt throbbing at the jarring impact with the hard earth, just as much as my forehead smarted from connecting with his skull. Mills recovered before I could gain my feet, his face enraged, an angry red lump on his forehead, and throbbing veins told me he was not pleased.

He charged at me, throwing himself on top of me and forcing me onto my back. My breath whooshed out, and I struggled to draw a breath from the sheer weight of him. I wheezed in disbelief, my lungs protesting. Mills' hands closed around my neck and squeezed, his eyes manic as he held his face inches from mine while I kicked, bucked, and writhed beneath him, trying to break free. He was heavy, and I was running out of air. Above the ringing in my ears, I could hear Anita screaming, and Ben yelling, and the revelation that I was in serious trouble brought my own mortality into stark focus. Mills wasn't messing about. He intended to kill me, consequences be damned. It was up to me how I went out, and this wasn't it, no way I'd let this douche take me down without a fight.

Think, Audrey, think. But it was difficult with a distinct lack of oxygen. I stopped thrashing around; it was achieving nothing. My slight build could not dislodge his heavier one. He had the upper hand, but I wasn't done yet. I dropped my hands that had been clawing at his wrists and felt along the ground, scratching into the earth. A rock. Anything that I could use as a weapon.

"On your left." Ben crouched by my head. "There's a rock to your left. You've almost got it."

I felt around blindly, my fingers finally finding the rock and closing around it. It wasn't big, but I didn't need big, I just needed hard. I swung, heard the sickening crunch as it connected with the side of his head. The pressure eased on my neck. With my other hand, I scooped up a handful of dirt and tossed it into his face. He reared back, hands going to his eyes. Bucking my hips with all my might, I managed to dislodge him. As he toppled to his side, I crawled away, gasping in great gulps of air, ignoring the dirt and gravel that dug into my palms and knees. Rather that than be dead.

"What the hell is going on?" Clements shouted from the porch.

"Oh my, Audrey, are you all right?" Anita crouched by my side, her hand on my back, giving me icy chills. It was actually quite soothing, considering my burning lungs.

"She attacked me!" Mills spat dirt from his mouth, and I grunted in satisfaction. Despite being clumsy, it seems I had a pretty good aim after all.

"She attacked you?" I watched warily as Clements stepped down from the porch and headed towards Mills, grabbing him by the arm and helping him to his feet. There was an egg-shaped lump on his forehead, and blood matted his hair where I'd beamed him with the rock. The front of his uniform was covered in dirt.

Ben stood protectively in front of me while the two men conferred. My ears were still ringing, but I thought I heard Clements say, "you're on your own with this one."

"Galloway's here," Ben said over his shoulder. Sure enough, I made out the sound of an approaching car. Not sure my legs would hold me yet, I moved onto my butt and sat, hands dangling from my knees, head bent as I concentrated on breathing. In and out. In and out. Once I'd caught my breath, I clambered to my feet. I stood, hands-on-hips, watching as the two police officers warily eyeballed Galloway as he approached.

"What's going on?" He demanded, eyeing Mills' disheveled state. Clements took a step back and raised his hands in the air, physically and metaphorically distancing himself from Mills. Mills' eyes shifted to me, and Galloway turned to look.

"Audrey?" His long legs ate up the ground, and in two seconds flat, he was in front of me, big hands cupping my face and tilting my head up for a thorough inspection. I could only imagine I had a matching red mark on my forehead from the headbutt, and my T-shirt was torn. Galloway released me. Taking a step back, he looked me up and down. I stood and waited.

"Don't freak out," I warned him, knowing the conclusions he was coming too. "You need to do this by the book for it to stick. And we must make it stick, okay?"

His jaw worked, but no words came out. There was a distinct tremble in his hands when he reached for mine, but rather than comforting me, he examined my nails. I almost gagged when I saw what was under them. Flesh. Mills flesh. Under my nails. I didn't remember scratching him, but apparently, I had, maybe when I was clawing at his wrists.

Anita and Ben had fallen silent, gathering in close, closing ranks against Mills, who was most likely realizing how very screwed he was. Galloway's eyes were focused on my neck. "Does it hurt?" His voice came out like he'd been chewing gravel. I reached a hand to my neck reflexively. The skin was tender to touch, no doubt bruised from where Mills had tried to strangle me.

"It's fine." I lied. "Galloway," I warned, seeing the murderous gleam in his eyes. "Kade." I tried again, using his first name. "Do not lose your shit. I need you to keep your shit together. Otherwise, I just might lose my shit, and then we really will be in the shit."

Ben snorted. "Eloquent, Fitz."

"I'm doing my best." He ground out, voice low so only I could hear. "I just need a minute; otherwise, I will pulverize that bastard. He deserves worse."

I nodded, reached out, and slid my arms around his waist and hugged him. His arms wrapped around me, returning the embrace. "He'll get worse. He crossed the line today, and I'm the physical evidence of that. I'm sure I heard Clements say he's on his own with this one."

"Did he witness it?"

I shook my head. "He was inside. I'm assuming you called? It sent Mills into a rage. He came storming outside, straight for me, told me he was sick of me interfering, grabbed my T-shirt, and lifted me off the ground. I head-butted him." Galloway sniggered at that part. "But I lost my footing when he released me, and I guess he took advantage of that for the next thing I knew he was sitting on me, strangling me." I squeezed Galloway's waist tight when I felt his muscles shift and tense, knew he wanted nothing more than to beat the ever-living snot out of Mills.

"I'm okay, I promise," I reassured him. "We need to

remember what we're here for. Anita Finley is dead, and I'm pretty sure she was murdered."

Galloway sucked in a deep breath and slowly released it, his body relaxing in my arms. We disengaged, and he took a step back, putting some distance between us. "Right. First, I need to deal with Mills. We need another crew out here. Are you okay, do you need medical attention?"

"I'm fine, just bruised." I smiled, an overly bright smile, showing all my teeth.

"Stop snarling at him, Fitz," Ben said.

"I'm not snarling, I'm smiling," I protested.

"Maybe dial it down a notch."

"Ben's here?" Galloway guessed, looking around as if he might catch a glimpse of him. I nodded. "And, Anita."

Galloway's head jerked in surprise. "She's here?"

"Mmmhmm." I glanced over at Clements and Mills, who were watching us, no doubt wondering what we were whispering about. "You go deal with..." I waved a hand in their direction. "Then we can talk about Anita. And her murder."

CHAPTER SIX

Officer Sarah Jacobs scraped the skin cells I'd inadvertently collected from Mills into an evidence bag, photographed my bruised neck and torn T-shirt, and took my statement. "Are you going to press charges?" She asked. I looked at her like she'd grown a second head. "Hell yeah, I'm pressing charges." As if I wouldn't. Mills had taken things a step too far, and finally, finally, he'd be made accountable.

She nodded, packing up her kit. "Good. Okay, we're all done here. I'll type up your statement. We'll need you to drop into the station to go through it one more time and sign it, but we have everything we need to begin a preliminary investigation."

"And Mills? What happens to him in the meantime?"

I hadn't seen him since Jacobs and Young had

turned up, followed by another squad car with Sergeant Powell and Officer Collier. Officer Jacobs lowered her voice. "Both he and Clements have been sent back to the station. This is big, Audrey. And bad. What he did to you? Totally not okay."

"What do you think will happen to him?"

"He should be kicked off the force for this. But I'd say they'll suspend him while it's investigated. That's what I'd do, anyway." She sniffed, then placed a comforting hand on my arm. "I'm so sorry he did this to you. It's inexcusable."

"Agreed." I nodded. "So, we're all done now?"

"You're free to go." Picking up her kit, she swiveled on her heel and made her way back to her squad car, securing the kit in the trunk. I texted Galloway. He was up in the attic, examining the crime scene.

Heading off. See you at mine later?

His response was immediate. *You got it. I'll cook.*

With a smile, I returned to my car, Ben and Anita in tow.

"What now?" Anita asked.

"The ME will do a postmortem examination to confirm the cause of death," I replied absently.

"No, not that. I mean you. Us. Now, what do we do?"

"Oh! Well, first, we're going back to my place." I maneuvered my car out of its parking spot, careful not to ding Anita's car in front of me, nor the patrol car parked behind me. "I want to examine what we have so far."

"Oh, good. When Officer Jacobs said you were free to go, I thought she meant, you know, go. As in go away. Do nothing."

"Doing nothing is not in my genes." I grinned.

"You know what's in her genes?" Ben chimed in. "Being clumsy. Audrey here has to be the clumsiest person you'll ever meet." The rear camera alert began beeping, screeching a warning that I was in imminent danger of a collision. I shifted into drive and continued to execute the world's worst seventy-six-point turn. All the while, Ben regaled Anita with tales of my escapades, which had her in stitches of laughter. I ignored them both and concentrated on getting my car out of its tight spot without damaging it. Also, with a team of cops currently swarming the Kelsh estate, I didn't need to get busted holding an animated conversation with my empty cab.

"Oh, good. You're home. About my bowl." Thor greeted me at the door, winding around my ankles and almost tripping me up.

"Don't tell me. It's empty?"

"Very astute, human." He sniffed, tail in the air as he waddled his way ahead of me to the living area at the rear of the house. I eyed his round belly and wondered if I needed to put the adorable British shorthair cat I'd inherited from Ben on a diet. Maybe I needed to stop filling his bowl at every "I'm starving" complaint? This was my first turn at pet ownership, and I had a sneaky suspicion Thor was training me and not the other way around.

"Actually, I brought something for you," I said.

"A treat?" He said hopefully.

"Yes. A treat. But I want you to use your feline skills and tell me if there's any seafood in it. Can you do that?"

"Of course!"

I knelt on the floor and unwrapped the tissue containing the morsel of noodle cup I'd swiped from the attic. Thor approached and sniffed thoroughly. "Hmmm. Notes of chicken. I approve. But also, just the slightest hint of..." he paused, sniffed, then sat back on his haunches. "Fish," he declared.

"Really? You can smell fish?" I didn't want to get my hopes up, but it was looking like my theory just might be right.

"You doubt me?"

"No, not at all." I ruffled the fur on his head. "Here you go. Taste it. Just to be sure."

He ate the entire thing, then licked his lips, his tongue snaking out over his whiskers. "Not bad." He flicked his tail. "And I stand by my initial findings. Sauce. Oyster or fish. Not the real thing."

"But, there's no oyster sauce in Lacey's noodle cups." Anita sounded puzzled, and I glanced at her over my shoulder. "Not in her noodle cups, no. But in this one? Yes."

"You think someone spiked it?" Ben flopped down onto the sofa, one arm resting along the back.

I nodded. "I do. Whoever did this knew about your allergy and knew that you'd most likely take Lacey's noodle cups home as leftovers. And even if you didn't, if someone else ate them? No harm, no foul. It's you, specifically, that they targeted. Or, more precisely, your allergy. Anita? This was intentional. Someone set out to —" I almost said kill you, but softened it to, "harm you."

"Oh." Anita blinked, a stunned expression on her face. "But who would...? Why?"

"That's what we're here to find out." I headed into the kitchen and flicked on the coffeemaker. After the day I'd had if I could take my caffeine intravenously, I would. "Tell me about your movements. From last night onwards." I said over my shoulder.

"Yes, yes, of course." She chewed her lip and looked up at the ceiling. "Umm. So yes. Friday night. Well, it was the museum's annual dinner. Gosh, it feels so long ago already."

"Yes, the dinner." I encouraged with a smile. "Tell

me about the end of the evening, what time you left, who was there. What happened to the food?"

"Most people had gone by nine-thirty, ten. We encourage those who brought a shared plate to take any leftovers back home with them. Still, some don't bother, so Lacey and I stayed behind to sort that out and pack up the leftovers in Tupperware containers. But we binned Eleanor's seafood surprise. I'm so sorry about that, Audrey!"

"It's totally okay," I assured her. "So you and Lacey stayed back to pack-up leftover food. What did you do with it? Take it home?"

"No, we put it in the historical society's refrigerator. That way, the clean-up crew could snack on it if they wanted, and we could use it for lunches during the week if there was a lot."

"And was there much leftover?"

"Not really. Half a dozen of Lacey's noodle cups— she always makes extra—a handful of sandwiches, some muffins."

"Okay, so after you'd stored the leftovers in the fridge, then what?"

"We went home. Lacey and I were the last to leave. I locked up, walked to my car. Lacey got a call, so she waved goodbye. I saw her in my rearview, standing next to her car, talking on the phone as I drove away."

"What time did you get home?"

"Just after eleven. Logan was already in bed, asleep.

I assume Tyler was out with his friends. There wasn't a light on in his room, and if he were home, I'd see the glow under the door."

"And you went straight to bed?"

"I did. I was wiped out, I slept right through Logan getting up the next morning."

"You said he'd brought you a cup of tea?"

"He did. I usually wake up when he leaves. He brings me a cup of tea so I can enjoy it in bed. But I must have been more tired than I thought; by the time I woke up, the tea was cold."

"So you woke up, the tea was cold... what time was that? And then what did you do?"

"It was around eight-thirty. I got dressed and headed out."

"Breakfast?"

"I skipped it. I'd overslept, and I wanted to get out to the Kelsh estate and just get on with sorting that mess out."

"But you had Lacey's noodle cups with you. Did you take some home after all?"

"I stopped at the historical society on the way. I knew there were leftovers in the fridge, so I grabbed the noodle cups and then went out to the farm." She smiled wistfully. "Lacey knows they're my favorite, she deliberately makes extra, so I can have the leftovers."

I shot a look at Ben. "What is it?" He asked.

"The thing is, I called into the museum yesterday

morning looking for her. Keagan was there as part of the clean-up crew, and he said he hadn't seen Anita that morning."

"You're saying he lied?"

"Oh, he probably didn't see me." Anita cut in. "I didn't duck my head into the museum. I knew I'd get roped into helping if they knew I was there. I saw their cars out front, so I knew they had everything in hand."

"Oh." Darn. There went that theory.

I finished making my coffee and cradled the cup in my hands while my mind went over the events leading up to Anita's death. Ben, who was still lounging on the sofa, cleared his throat, and I glanced at him.

"I hate to say this," he began.

"Then don't." I cut him off with a teasing smile.

"Ha-ha." He leaned forward, resting his elbows on his knees and pinning Anita with an intent gaze. "I hate to say this," he repeated, "but nine out of ten cases, the spouse did it."

Anita's hand fluttered to her throat. "You're saying Logan killed me?" The incredulity in her voice was unmistakable.

"It's possible," Ben said.

"Tell me about the supposed affair," I said, taking a sip of the brew and burning my lip on the scalding liquid.

Anita rolled her eyes. "I already told you, I don't think Logan is having an affair. It was Lacey who said that, not me. I told her he's been distracted lately. Secretive. That I suspect he's keeping something from me. But I don't think he's having an affair."

"Distracted and secretive?" I ticked off on my fingers. "What do you think it is, if not an affair?"

Anita deflated, her shoulders rolling forward and her chin dropping to her chest. "I don't know." She mumbled, but I don't think it's an affair... it can't be."

Ben and I shared a look. Maybe Anita was burying her head in the sand, and who could blame her? But she said it herself. Her husband was behaving strangely. And now Anita was dead.

"We need to speak to Logan," I said, blowing on my coffee to cool it before risking another layer of skin being removed from my lip.

"It's not him." Anita crossed her arms over her chest and planted her feet. I recognized the stance. She'd snapped out of disbelief and misery and had moved on to stubborn and defiant.

"Maybe it isn't, but you said yourself. He wasn't himself. That you thought he was keeping something from you. We need to find out what so we can eliminate him from our investigation."

She eyeballed me for a solid minute while she mulled over what I'd said. I continued to blow on my coffee before taking a tentative sip. Ahhh. Bearable. Drinkable. I bolted down a mouthful and promptly choked as the liquid went down the wrong hole.

Snorting coffee out of my nose, I set the cup down on the counter while coughing up a storm.

"You okay, Fitz?" I felt the icy chill where Ben patted my back. I held up a hand and waved him away. I'd be fine once I could draw a breath into my coffee-soaked lungs. Eventually, I got my coughing fit under control and wiped my fingers under my eyes, blinking rapidly to disperse the watering.

"Oh, my!" Anita fluttered around me. "Are you okay, Audrey?"

"Sorry." I croaked, clearing my throat. "Went down the wrong way. I'm just going to change my shirt, and then we'll go see Logan."

CHAPTER SEVEN

For the second time that day, I pulled up out the front of the Finley house. This time a truck sat in the driveway with a Finley Construction decal on the door. I turned to look at Anita, who was sitting in the back seat.

"Okay?" I asked. I knew the police had already informed Logan of his wife's death. I'd thought at the time that Anita would have left the crime scene to join her husband, but she'd elected to stay with Ben and me. This would be her first meeting with her husband and son since she'd died.

She was looking at her house, a craftsman style bungalow that was clearly well cared for. "Yes." She eventually said and stepped through the car door. Ben followed, while I went the more conventional route and opened my door. The two of them waited behind me while I knocked, and I thought about how odd it was for Anita to be outside with us when she could have just walked through. I cast a quick glance at her over my shoulder. She looked pale. But then, she was a ghost, of course, she looked pale. But she was twisting her fingers together and chewing her bottom lip. I guess I'd be agitated too if I'd just turned up dead, and everyone thought my husband was the killer. Not that I have a husband.

The door swung open, and Tyler Finley scowled at me.

"What do you want? Now isn't a good time." He was pale, his eyes red-rimmed.

"Who is it, Tyler?" A male voice called, then a tall man with a shock of silver hair appeared behind him. It had to be Logan, his father, the family resemblance was impossible to miss.

"Mr. Finley? Hi, I'm Audrey Fitzgerald, I was working with your wife." I cleared my throat. "Actually, I was the one who found her."

Logan's lips trembled, then firmed into a hard line. "You'd better come in." He held the door wider, and Tyler spun on his heel without a word, retreating upstairs.

"I'm so sorry for your loss," I said, stepping inside.

"Thank you," Logan replied. "We're in the living room. To your right."

We turned out to be Lacey Stevens, Keagan Dunn,

and Noreen Bellamy, all sitting side by side on the sofa, cups of tea in hand. Lacey jumped to her feet and offered me her seat. "Audrey, please, sit. Tea? Coffee?"

"Coffee would be great." After Lacey had left for the kitchen, I turned my attention to Keagan and Noreen next to me. "Word travels fast."

"In a town this size?" Keagan said. "Undoubtedly. We—" he indicated Noreen sitting to his left, "were just leaving the museum when we heard. We came straight here."

"Right. And Lacey? She was part of the clean-up crew, too, wasn't she?" Although she hadn't turned up when I dropped by earlier.

"She was meant to be," Noreen sniffed. "But she didn't show. Keagan and I, as he said, came straight here. Imagine our surprise to find Lacey already here. We thought maybe she'd been called into a shift at the hotel, but apparently not." There was a distinct note of disapproval in Noreen's voice. I shot a glance at Ben, who was standing behind Logan's chair. He shrugged. I wondered what Lacey had been up to this morning while her best friend was dying. She certainly hadn't been where she was meant to be.

Logan cleared his throat. "You said you found Anita?" His hands trembled as he reached for his coffee cup. Anita, who'd been absently gazing around her own living room, moved closer to him.

"Oh, darling." She cooed, touching his arm. He jerked, no doubt feeling the icy coldness of her touch.

"Yes," I answered, then glanced at Keagan and Noreen, who was practically holding their breath, waiting to hear the juicy details. "Maybe you'd prefer to discuss this in private?" I suggested. Logan jerked his head toward the couple on the sofa, as if he'd forgotten they were even there.

"Private. Yes, yes, that might be best." He agreed.

"Oh. Well, yes, of course." Noreen immediately set her teacup down on the coffee table in front of the sofa and got to her feet, patted Logan's arm, and let herself out, Keagan hot on her heels.

Lacey returned with my coffee just as the others were leaving. Placing the drink on the coffee table in front of me, she addressed Logan. "Is everything okay?"

I answered for him. "Logan and I just need a chat in private. If you don't mind?" I raised an eyebrow and cocked my head toward the front door.

Lacey eyeballed me for a second, then smiled. "I'll just go say goodbye to Tyler." She rested her hand on Logan's arm then headed upstairs to what I presumed was Tyler's bedroom. The stairs creaked under her weight. Anita, who'd been standing in the doorway watching, wandered into the kitchen. Ben remained behind Logan's armchair. I did my best to ignore both of them.

"You wanted to talk?" Logan prompted.

"Yes. As I said, I'm Audrey Fitzgerald... I'm a private investigator. I wasn't actually here to help Anita with the Kelsh estate. She hired me for something else."

He blanched. "She hired you? What for?"

"To find her missing necklace."

He deflated back against his chair as if relieved. I narrowed my eyes. Had Lacey been on the money after all, and Logan was having an affair?

"That darn thing? I'm sorry she wasted your time with it." He said.

"It was important to her," I replied. "She was convinced someone had stolen it."

"I don't know why someone would steal it. It wasn't worth anything."

"It had great sentimental value to her." I reminded him.

"Yeah. It did." He looked up at the ceiling, his bloodshot eyes filling with tears. "I should have paid more attention. Should have helped her look for it. The truth is, it's probably lost—it had a funny clasp, and I'd told her I'd take it in to get it fixed... but I never did. And now it's gone, and so is she." He ended on a sob, burying his face in his hands. I glanced at Ben, at a loss to know what to do.

Ben shrugged. "Give him a minute to compose himself." He suggested, so I waited in silence until Logan straightened, running his hands over his face.

"The police said it was her allergy," Logan said, prompting me to get on with why I was here.

I nodded. "It looks that way. I was meant to have a meeting with Anita this morning, but it seems we got our wires crossed about where. I came here first, then the historical society, and finally out to the Kelsh estate."

"Where you found her."

"Where I found her." I agreed. "Can you tell me about her allergy?"

"She had a severe seafood allergy." Logan sniffed, eyes glassy. "Deadly. She couldn't have anything with seafood in it, not even a whiff."

"Right. So I assume she had medication? In case she accidentally ingested anything that would trigger her allergy?"

"Oh yeah, her EpiPen. That thing was always with her."

"Has she had to use it? Recently?"

"Not for a while." Logan chewed his lip as he thought back. "Maybe six months ago? She'd grabbed a sandwich from Grille 19, that trendy place on Sugar Maple Lane? Anyway, yeah, she thinks maybe the chopping board or knife they used must've been contaminated, because she'd only had a couple of mouthfuls of her ham and cheese croissant when she felt the first signs."

"Which are?"

"Tingling lips and fingers. Then a feeling like it's hard to swallow, hard to breathe. That's because her airways are closing up, and her tongue is swelling." He added.

"Then what happened?"

"She pulled her EpiPen out of her purse and gave herself a shot in the leg."

"Did she go to the hospital?"

He shook his head. "No need. She was fine. She called me to come pick her up and spent the rest of the day resting here at home. She was right as rain in the morning."

"Have you ever had to administer the EpiPen?" I asked.

"Yes. Tyler too. She dragged us to an education evening once, when Tyler was a kid, so we'd know what to do if she ever had an attack and wasn't able to do it herself. It's not hard to do, though. You just press and click." He mimicked the action on his leg. "Straight through clothes if you have to." He huffed out a breath then smiled slightly. "Poor Tyler. It kinda freaked him out. He was only nine or ten. After that evening, he insisted he had an EpiPen too, just in case his mom ever needed it and didn't have her purse. She got him one, and he carried it in his backpack right up until he finished school. I wouldn't be surprised if he still had one stashed somewhere."

I watched the ebb and flow of emotions as they

crossed Logan's face. He was clearly distraught. Ben had been convinced Logan was the killer, but I wasn't so sure.

"You weren't at the Museum's annual dinner Friday night," I said into the silence that had fallen. "Did you see Anita when she got home?"

"Urgh," he groaned. "Those things are so boring! Thankfully, Anita stopped dragging me along a couple of years ago."

Anita strolled through from the kitchen back into the living room, making me jump. "He tried valiantly for such a long time." She sighed with a soft smile on her face, crossing to stand beside Logan's armchair. "But he's right, he was bored out of his mind, so I let him off the hook. Truth be told, I had a better time without him hovering, asking me every ten minutes if we could go yet."

"Did you see her before she left for the dinner?" I asked.

"Yes. I kissed her goodbye, told her to have fun." Logan said.

"Yes, he did." Anita echoed, smiling fondly at her husband.

"And what about when she got home? What time was that?"

"I'm not sure. I was already in bed, I sort of half woke up when she climbed into bed, but I didn't look at the clock or anything."

"It was just after eleven, darling," Anita said. "Lacey and I got to chatting while we were packing up the leftovers, we were the last to leave. And Logan, bless him, he'd have dozed off in front of the tv by eight-thirty and dragged himself up to bed by ten."

I made a note in my phone, and Ben glanced at me. I returned his look, deadpan. "Did you see her this morning?"

A flash of grief contorted his features, and my heart jerked in response. "No. I had a quote for a job, so I was up early, and because she got in late, I didn't want to disturb her. She was still asleep when I left."

"He left me a cup of tea," Anita said softly. "Of course, it was stone cold by the time I woke up, but it's the thought that counts." A man who was supposedly having an affair wouldn't stop and make his sleeping wife a cup of tea before he slipped out of the house for an early morning tryst, would he? I reminded myself that Anita didn't think her husband was having an affair, it was her best friend, Lacey, who was pushing that agenda.

"What time was that?"

"I left at seven-thirty. I was meeting my potential client at eight, but I wanted to swing by the construction yard first."

"And did you know what her movements were? Her plans for the day?"

"The usual. Swing by the museum and make sure

the cleaning crew had turned up even though she wasn't rostered on. Then out to the Kelsh estate. She'd been really excited finding that painting, despite Dunn telling her it was worthless, that Kelshs' grandparents or great grandparents must have dabbled in painting at one time or another. Still, it meant a lot to Anita, so she insisted he take it and clean it up so they could hang it, if not in the museum, then in the historical society itself. Anyway, I think she was hoping for more discoveries like that, she was determined to go through every item out there and document it, even if it ended up in Goodwill or the trash."

"I didn't think you were listening." Anita sighed wistfully, then glanced at me. "I'd come home and blabber on about the Kelsh estate and fill him in on my finds, and he'd nod and say, 'that's nice dear,' and I didn't think he was listening. But he was."

"How long would she stay at the Kelsh estate?"

"All day if she didn't have anything else on. Anita is the type who would push through and get a job done, so if she had the time, she'd stay there until sundown. But not once it got dark. She said it was spooky out there with no street lights." He chuckled at the memory.

"Was anyone helping her? At the Kelsh estate? Would anyone else have been out there?"

"Now that I don't know. She didn't mention anyone. I think the committee was more than happy for Anita to do the lion's share of the work. I haven't been out there myself, but from what I hear, it's a dump."

"Did she have any visitors? Here, at the house, before she headed out?"

"I wouldn't know. I was gone before she got up, and when I got home, she'd left. Tyler was home, he might know."

The creaking of the stairs heralded Tyler's arrival. "Might know what?" He asked, appearing in the doorway.

"Did anyone call in to visit with your mum this morning?" Logan repeated the question.

Tyler screwed up his face. "Not that I know of. But then I slept until after midday, so... dunno."

"He's out all night, sleeps all day." Anita admonished, tsking around her son, who was oblivious to her presence. "But no, no-one dropped in."

I frowned. "Umm. I called in just before ten, remember? You were up and dressed."

"You woke me up!"

I cocked my head and studied him. When Tyler had opened the door this morning, he did not look like he'd just dragged himself out of bed. He looked wide awake, alert, and groomed as if he had been expecting someone.

"Interesting," Ben said, following my train of thought.

"You don't work on Saturdays?" I asked, letting the lie slide for now.

Tyler shrugged. "Used to. My hours were cut."

"I told you, Ty, it's not personal. Everyone's hours were cut. Business has been slow. At least you've got a roof over your head." Logan snapped. Anita started fussing over the two of them. "Boys, boys, let's not start this up again. It'll work out. We've had dips before, it's the industry. Business will pick up."

"And you didn't hear from your mom at all this morning?" I confirmed.

"Nope. I figured she was out at the Kelsh place. She was obsessed with it, ever since finding that painting. She seemed to think it was some sort of big deal, but Keagan says it's amateurish doodling and not worth anything. Too bad. Woulda been nice for Mom to find something nice out there after all the hard work she put in. None of the other hysterical society could be bothered."

I snorted at his nickname for the historical society. Hysterical indeed.

"Jokes on them though, they're going to have to get off their lazy asses now that she's dead," he continued, crossing his arms over his chest.

"Tyler!" Anita scolded, then rolled her eyes. "Don't mind him. He's at that age where he doesn't like anybody." I glanced at Ben, who looked as surprised as I felt. Anita was talking about Tyler as if he was a fifteen-year-old going through a phase. He was twenty years old, would be twenty-one soon, and a fully-fledged adult. At least on paper if not in brain cells.

"Tyler, you haven't seen your mom's necklace around, have you?" I changed tack.

"Oh my God, not you too! Christ, Mom wouldn't stop going on about it. She lost it. End of story. What does it matter now, anyway?" His voice rose several octaves, and a flush of red swept across his cheekbones.

"Okay, look, I think that's enough for today," Logan said, pushing himself up out of the armchair and sliding a comforting arm around his son's shoulders. I hastily scrambled to my feet.

"Thanks for your time." I shook Logan's hand. "Once again, sorry for your loss," I added, stepping out into the hallway, following Ben to the front door. I almost walked through him when he stopped and looked up. There on the landing was Lacey Stevens. I'd forgotten she was still in the house. She's said she was going upstairs to say goodbye to Tyler, why hadn't she left when he came downstairs? Was she eavesdropping?

Ben stepped aside, giving me a clear path to the front door. "You go ahead." He said as I passed him. "I'm going to hang here with Anita for a bit, see what, if anything, turns up." He was staring straight at Lacey.

I nodded slightly, clamping my lips together to bite

back the urge to reply before turning the doorknob and stepping outside. Good plan. There was something about Lacey that set my spidey senses tingling. She was the one who'd planted the idea of an affair in Anita's head. What if the person Logan was having an affair with, was Lacey herself? And who better placed to find out the truth than a ghost?

CHAPTER EIGHT

"*T*ell me again." I sat curled up on the sofa, a glass of wine in hand. Galloway was in the kitchen, preparing dinner. Galloway, it turns out, is a superb cook, which is another tick in the plus column since I'm somewhat domestically challenged. Really, when I looked at it on paper, Galloway was getting a bum deal with me. Not that he seemed to mind.

"Really?" Thor meowed in protest. "He's already told you once." The cat stretched, his back dipping low and long before he straightened again. "This Mills character has been suspended pending review. That's good news, right?"

I chuckled and snapped my fingers. Thor trotted over to head bump my hand. "It is excellent news," I said, scratching his head.

"You want some chicken?" Galloway asked, slicing

off a morsel for Thor and holding it up. I'd never seen Thor move so fast; he was in the kitchen wrapping himself around Galloway's ankles in two seconds flat. "Chicken!" He purred. "My favorite."

I snorted. "Steak was your favorite yesterday. Before that, fish."

"Hey," Thor protested, "I'm a feline of many tastes."

"Here you go, buddy. Enjoy." Galloway dropped the chicken to the floor and ruffled Thor's fur before straightening and returning to carving the roast he'd prepared for dinner. "Is Ben here?"

"No. He and Anita are at her house." Sometimes it came in handy having a ghost as a best friend. Ben's plan to hang around and see what developed at the Finley house was a win-win. For one, anything they saw or heard could lead us to the killer, and two, Galloway and I had the place to ourselves.

"Earth to Audrey." Galloway's teasing jerked me back to the present.

"Sorry, I was daydreaming." I took another sip of wine.

"Reliving today?" He was referring to my run-in with Mills, and not my visit with Logan, which I hadn't told him about because I knew what he'd say. Stay out of an active police investigation. Therefore, what he didn't know, wouldn't get me in trouble.

"How did you know?"

"The frown, then the smile." He grinned.

"I won't lie, despite being sat on by that fat bastard, I'm not sorry it happened. If it means getting Mills off the force, it was worth it."

Galloway picked up two plates loaded with roast chicken and all the trimmings and carried them to the dining table. "Dinner's ready."

"Thanks so much for doing this." Joining him at the table, I set my glass down, only it was half on, half off the placemat and it began to teeter. Galloway shot out a hand and rescued it. "I'm starting to think I should keep you around." I grinned, taking my seat.

"I'm starting to think that sounds like an excellent idea." He shot back with a wink. My heart stuttered in my chest, then resumed its beating at double time. I was still shell-shocked. I was in a relationship with a cop. Even more so that I'd put a label on it. Kade Galloway was officially my boyfriend. I hadn't had a boyfriend in forever. But Captain Cowboy Hot Pants currently sitting across from me, playing footsie under the table, had wormed his way under my defenses and torn down the wall I'd built around my heart. I was equally terrified and totally smitten.

Thor jumped up onto the chair at the end of the table and rested his paws on the tabletop. "I'm starving." He meowed, adopting what I called his Puss in Boots expression to elicit treats.

"You are not starving." I admonished but sliced him off a tiny piece of chicken and placed it in front of him. He snatched it up in his jaws and jumped to the floor to devour it. "So glad Ben isn't here to see me do that."

"He doesn't approve?" Galloway chuckled.

"Nope. Cat food goes in cat bowls, and cats should most definitely not be sitting at the table." The first time Thor had joined me at the table, I'd been eating cereal for breakfast, and I'd thought it was the cutest thing. We'd come to an agreement. Thor could sit on a chair, and he could rest his front paws on the tabletop, but he couldn't climb all the way onto the table. It was a compromise we could both work with. Ben, however, had almost had a fit.

"So what happens next, with Mills?" I asked once we'd finished eating and were clearing the table. No-one at the Kelsh estate had given me a straight answer today.

"Both he and Clements are under investigation. Mills is suspended with pay for now." Galloway said, rinsing a plate then stacking it in the dishwasher. "We have to wait and see what the outcome is."

"We can make this stick, right?" I chewed my bottom lip. "He can't wriggle out of this?"

"It damn well better," Galloway growled. "It helps that I was on the scene immediately after it happened. I was an eyewitness to your injuries—and his."

"Is that going to be an issue? That I hurt him?"

"You were defending yourself. The fact that you

had to defend yourself against an officer of the law makes my blood boil."

I sidled up to him and slid my arms around his waist, then squeezed his butt. "I can think of better ways to make your blood boil." I teased suggestively, and he laughed, lifting me onto the kitchen bench and wedging himself between my legs.

"Oh, yeah?" He dropped soft kisses against my neck, carefully placing one on each and every bruise. "Like what?"

"Well, Mills attack may have left bruises... in other places." I hinted. "Wanna check?" I eased back a little and pulled my T-shirt over my head.

"I do believe I can be of assistance with that." He drawled, hands skimming over my bra, spanning my ribs and sliding around to my back, searching for the clasp.

The ringing of his phone couldn't have come at a worse time. I snorted out a disbelieving laugh. "That had better be important," I grumbled. He heaved a sigh and lifted his head, reached into his pocket for his phone, and glanced at the screen. I arched one brow. Fine. It was both brows.

"It's the medical examiner."

"Better get it then." I picked up my T-shirt and pulled it back on. Something told me this particular phone call would be a mood killer.

Galloway kept the phone to his ear, listening to the

medical examiner while sliding his arm around my waist and easing me off the bench. When I moved to step away, he pinned me against him, shaking his head.

"Got it." He said into the phone while I leaned against him. "Yep. Thanks for the call, appreciate it." Then he hung up.

"Well?"

"No surprises that Anita died from anaphylaxis, triggered by her seafood allergy."

"And the noodle cups? Did they contain seafood?"

"This is where it gets interesting. The lab sampled all the noodle cups. None of them contained seafood. Not even a trace."

"Oh." That was puzzling. Because the piece I'd brought home for Thor had. Well, at least Thor thought so. Maybe his taste buds were defective.

"Except for the one found in her hand." He added. I jerked my head up.

"Really?"

He laughed. "You're not meant to sound happy about it."

I punched him in the arm. "You know what I mean. This was intentional. Someone spiked a noodle cup, knowing she was allergic! I'm right, aren't I?" I didn't tell him I was already up and running with that theory.

He squeezed me tight. "It's looking like that, Sherlock." Releasing me, he turned to the coffee machine. "Better tell me what you got up to today,

Fitz." His back was to me while he prepped the machine, so he missed the sight of my jaw dropping open.

"What do you mean?" I knew what he meant, but I was buying time.

He snorted. "Don't tell me you weren't investigating Anita's death. I'm not that naïve."

I sucked my lips in, releasing them with a popping noise. "Okay, then."

He threw me a look over his shoulder, his eyes twinkling with laughter. "Come on. Spill. Who knows, you may save me some time with my investigation."

"What are you suggesting, Detective?" I cocked my head. "That we pool resources?"

"Not the worst idea."

I studied his broad shoulders, then his tight butt encased in denim, my mind wandering until he swiveled at the waist and snapped his fingers under my nose. "Eyes up here, Fitz," he teased, then dropped a kiss on my cheek. "But seriously. Your exam is Monday. That gives us oh, about thirty-six hours to solve this case, so you're not distracted. Plus, we have to carve out some time for your family dinner."

My eyes narrowed. Family dinner?

"Did I forget to mention your mom called me today?" he said, feigning innocence. "Inviting me to family dinner. Tomorrow night."

I gasped, hand to my chest. "She didn't!"

His smile was full-blown. "She did."

"The rat," I grumbled. I still wasn't sure I was ready to subject Galloway to my family. I'm not sure what worried me most, that they'd scare him off with all the horrendous stories they'd saved up for such an occasion, or they'd go overboard in their approval of him and have us married off and picking out china patterns before the meal was over. Neither option was appealing.

"Why are you so bothered over this?" Wrapping a hand around my nape, he massaged my neck, the long soothing strokes of his fingers working magic on my tense muscles.

"I'm not." I lied.

"I can cancel if you don't want them to meet me."

"My mom would never let you cancel. And it's not that I don't want them to meet you. It's more... I'm not sure I'm ready to subject you to them. They can be a bit full-on."

He snorted. "I can handle full-on. But if you really don't want me to come..."

Now I felt like a heel. "It's fine. Please come. I suppose I have to get it over with, eventually."

He barked out a laugh. "Like ripping off a band-aid?"

"A lot like that." I conceded. He turned his attention back to the coffee machine. "Tell me what you got up to this afternoon after you left the Kelsh farm."

I filled him in on my trip to the Finley house, how Keagan, Lacey, and Noreen were already there, and my theory on Lacey.

"And Ben and Anita are there now?" Galloway handed me my coffee, then waited for me to precede him to the sofa.

"Yeah. When I was leaving, I caught Lacey eavesdropping on the upstairs landing. At least I assume that's what she was doing. When the others left, rather than leaving, she said she was going upstairs to say goodbye to Tyler. Then he came downstairs without her. I didn't really give her a moment's thought, to be honest, but then I looked up as I was heading out, and she was there."

"So you've pegged Lacey as a suspect?" Galloway took a sip of his coffee and watched me over the brim.

"She's on my list. Anita told me it was Lacey who kept saying she thought Logan was having an affair. Anita didn't think he was, but she knew something was bothering him. But I can't help but wonder, after I saw how affectionate and comfortable Lacey was with Logan, touching his arm, going upstairs to say goodbye to Tyler, how close she was with the family, that maybe it was Lacey Logan was having an affair with. If he is even having an affair."

"You've jumped back and forth on that. What does your gut tell you?"

"That he was a man devastated at the loss of his wife. He was a bit shell shocked. And he didn't pay Lacey any attention. Despite her touching his arm and being domestic, for want of a better word, it all went over his head. What if Lacey had feelings for Logan, but they weren't reciprocated? So Lacey hatched a plan to get rid of what she saw as her competition? Get rid of the wife, insinuate herself into Logan's life, eventually win him over."

Galloway nodded, face grim. "Plausible. What does Ben think?"

"He says nine times out of ten, it's the husband or wife who murdered their spouse."

"Yeah, but that's just statistics. Does he have anything to back that up? A suspicion? Did he see something? Hear something? Find something?"

I sighed. "We have nothing other than speculation. But—" I held up a finger, "I think I caught Keagan out in a lie."

"Oh?"

"Yeah. I dropped by the museum slash historical society to look for Anita this morning, and he said he hadn't seen her. Only she'd called in on the way out to the Kelsh estate. But," I gnawed on my lower lip, "she did admit they may not have seen her, that she didn't stick her head in and say hello."

"Why did she call in there?"

I looked at him with wide eyes. "To pick up the noodle cups."

He leaned forward, eyes intent. "Lemme get this straight. Anita and Lacey were last to leave last night. And they stored the noodle cups in the fridge, yes?"

"Yes."

"And this morning, Keagan was at the museum, cleaning up, I assume?"

"Yes. Him and Noreen. Lacey was meant to be there too, but apparently, she didn't turn up."

Drumming his fingers against his lips, Galloway mulled over everything I'd told him. "Okay, so motive aside, let's look at opportunity. The noodle cups must have been tampered with either last night or this morning. Lacey didn't turn up this morning, which means, if it was her, she'd have had to do so last night."

"But Anita was with her the whole time." I pointed out.

"The whole time? You'd only need a minute or two to sprinkle oyster sauce onto a noodle cup. Could she have distracted Anita long enough to do that?"

I shot a look at Thor, who was curled up asleep in an armchair. Seems his taste buds had been spot on after all. Then I remembered what Anita had told me.

"They didn't leave together!" I leaned forward and slammed my cup down on the coffee table so hard the liquid sloshed over the rim. "Anita said they exited the building, locked up, but Lacey stopped to answer her phone. She was still in the parking lot when Anita drove away. She could have ducked back inside and administered the oyster sauce."

Galloway nodded. "So Lacey had the opportunity, but at this stage, no motive that we know about. What's also a little murky here is if Lacey is the guilty party, why spike her own noodle cups? She's pointing the finger at herself! She'd have been better off spiking something else. Okay, let's move on. Who was there this morning?"

"Keagan Dunn and Noreen Bellamy. And either one of them could have ducked next door and tampered with the noodle cups."

"So we have three suspects all with opportunity. What about Logan?"

"Opportunity? Well, I guess he could have ducked out in the middle of the night, taken Anita's keys, let himself into the historical society, spiked the noodle cups, then returned home, Anita none-the-wiser."

"Four suspects then. All with opportunity." Galloway paused.

"Right, so I guess we need to look at motive. And alibis. Narrow down our suspect pool."

"How do you suggest we go about that?" I knew he was testing me. Ordinarily, Galloway would guide me, but I have my private investigator exam coming up, and what better way to swat for it than to investigate a real murder?

"A couple of things kept coming up. One is that Logan is keeping a secret. Anita is absolutely convinced something was up with him, so we need to get to the bottom of that."

Galloway frowned. "You're saying you think the affair angle could be true?"

I shook my head. "No. I wouldn't be surprised if Lacey had a crush on him, but no, I'm trusting Anita's instincts on the affair front. What are the two things couples fight over?"

"You tell me."

I ticked them off on my fingers. "Money and sex. And if I temporarily shelve the sex angle, that leaves money. Tyler said his hours from the family business had been cut. Logan said business was slow. What if Logan was having money issues? Issues that he didn't want to worry his wife with. What if his business was in trouble?"

Galloway was nodding and pulling out his phone. "Good call. I'm going to get a warrant to go over his accounts and phone records." When he finished typing, he looked up at me. "You said two things?"

"Oh, yes. The other was the painting that Anita found at the Kelsh farm. Keagan, Logan, and Tyler all said the same thing—that it was amateur and worthless."

"You think differently?"

"It couldn't hurt to take a look for ourselves, right? Anita had been really excited about that find. What if the painting was actually worth something? Or, what if there was another treasure out at the farm and someone wanted to stop her from finding it? Dudley Kelsh left the contents of his estate to the historical society for a reason. It doesn't make sense that all he owns is worthless junk, there has to be something more to it."

Galloway slowly nodded, deep in thought. "Valid." Then he tossed his phone on the table. "We'll visit Dunn tomorrow and get a look at that painting for ourselves. And I've put in a subpoena for Logan's business and personal accounts."

"I can help with that—you know I'm a whiz at spreadsheets." I offered.

"Sounds like a plan." His lips curled in a wicked grin, and I knew his mind had gone from spreadsheets to bed sheets. Tugging me to my feet, he planted a hard kiss on my lips and growled, "about that body search?" I laughed and then squealed when he scooped me up in his arms and carried me upstairs.

CHAPTER NINE

Being woken up with a trail of soft kisses across your shoulder was something I could get used to. Stretching my arms over my head and arching my back off the mattress, I turned in Galloway's arms.

"Morning." I garbled through clenched lips. Galloway pulled back and stared at my face, brows puckered in a frown.

"What's wrong? Why do you sound funny?"

"Morning breath." I pointed at my mouth. "Lemme just go brush my teeth." He chuckled and nuzzled his face into my neck. "I don't care about morning breath. I'll just keep my face here... or lower."

I arched against him, my pulse picking up speed. "I like the sound of that." I purred.

"Are you two still in bed?" Ben asked from the foot

of the bed. I squealed and jerked the covers to my chin. Galloway sat up, searching the room for intruders.

"Ben!" I yelled. "Get out. The bedroom is off-limits." I could feel the heat in my face as embarrassment washed over me. What if we'd been... you know? And Ben had just come wandering in? Good Lord, having a ghost was worse than having kids. At least with small humans, you'd hear their footsteps and would have some semblance of warning. As it was, I'd had to keep the bedroom door shut to keep Thor from joining us. A situation he protested loudly about.

Galloway barked out a laugh and dropped back against the pillows. "Ben turned up, huh?"

I glared at Ben. "He certainly did. And now he's going to leave. Out!" I pointed to the door.

"Okay, okay, don't get your panties in a wad." Ben headed toward the door. "Oh wait, you're not wearing any!" He chortled at his own joke before disappearing.

Galloway turned his head to look at me. "Mood ruined?" I could tell by the hopeful tone in his voice that while he knew what my answer would be, he was hoping otherwise. Lifting my hand to his face, I gently patted his cheek. "Mood totally ruined."

After a shower, alone, and getting dressed, also alone, I followed my nose to the coffee I knew would be waiting for me. Sure enough, sitting on the kitchen counter was not only my coffee but Ben. Galloway was on a bar stool, flicking through his phone. Padding up to him on bare feet, I dropped a kiss on his bristly cheek and picked up my coffee. "News?" I asked.

"Warrant came through for Logan's financials."

"Cool, I can start going through them." I took a sip of coffee. There is nothing quite like that first kick of caffeine from your first coffee of the day. Well, nothing aside from morning sex, which Ben had put the dampeners on. I scowled at the ghost perched on the breakfast bar.

"Hey!" He protested, catching my look. "Don't get all mad at me, 'cos I interrupted your nookie."

"Nookie?" I snorted. "What are you, twelve?"

"I'm going to leave you to chat with Ben while I take a shower." Galloway stood and swatted my butt as he walked past.

"So?" I cocked my head, taking another sip of coffee. "Anything happen at the Finley's?"

Ben lifted one shoulder. "Nah. Other than the endless stream of neighbors dropping off food and condolences."

"Did Lacey leave?"

"She did. Just after you actually. Said she had to get ready for the evening shift at the hotel."

"You and Anita stayed there all night?" I glanced around, searching for the other ghost currently haunting me. "Where is she, by the way?"

"She's with Logan. He's pretty cut up."

"What do you think? Was he having an affair?"

"Hard to say. He is genuinely heartbroken that his wife is dead. But that doesn't mean he wasn't having an affair. Married men having affairs can still love their wives." I narrowed my eyes. I wasn't so sure about that. If you truly loved someone, you wouldn't cheat. Not in my book. And not in the books of most women I know, either.

"But Anita doesn't think so." I pointed out.

He shook his head. "No, she doesn't."

"What about Tyler? I caught him out in a lie yesterday. He said he slept till noon, but when I turned up at ten, he was up and dressed as if he were waiting for someone." I recalled the eager anticipation on his face when he'd opened the door, and the crushing disappointment when he discovered it was me and not whoever he'd been waiting for.

"He was on his phone most of the evening. Text messaging someone. I tried to get a look, but he was pretty secretive. He went out around midnight."

"Do you know where?"

"Nope. To hang with his friends, I presume. Logan had gone to bed; Anita and I were looking for her necklace—more as something to do than expecting to actually find it."

I chewed my lip. "That necklace bugs me. She's adamant she couldn't have lost it because the last time she saw it was in its jewelry box. Both Logan and Tyler mentioned the broken clasp, but it couldn't have fallen from her neck if she wasn't wearing it."

"You think someone stole it?" Ben looked at me in surprise.

"I'm saying I'm not ruling it out."

Ben jumped down from the counter and wandered to the back window, staring out at the garden and woods beyond. "Lawn needs mowing." He said absently.

"Yeah. I think I'll hire someone."

He looked at me over my shoulder. "Really? Why not do it yourself?"

"Time, for one. And I don't know how to use a mower." I admitted. I'd never mown grass in my life. Growing up, that had been my brother's or my dad's job. Not to mention the thought of whirling blades scared me. What if I lopped off a toe?

"Hire someone for what?" Galloway reappeared fresh from his shower, hair damp, smelling of my soap, and his own personal brand of sexiness.

"Mow the lawn."

"I'll do it." He offered, picking up my coffee and stealing a sip.

"Really?" I hadn't expected that, and my face must have shown my surprise. He chuckled and playfully bopped my chin with his knuckle. "Sure. What else do big brawny males do but mow lawns?"

I grinned. "Well, I could think of other things…"

"Ewwwwww." Ben screwed up his face. "You guys are the worst."

"Feel free to go and watch the shopping channel somewhere." I offered.

"That was a cheap shot, Fitz." Ben pouted, then winked, making me laugh. "Ask Galloway what the plan is for today."

I obliged. "Ben wants to know what the plan is for today?"

Galloway held up his hand and counted off on his fingers. "Visit Keagan Dunn's art gallery and get a look at that painting. Take a look at Finley's finances. Then dinner at the Fitzgerald's."

"Dinner with your folks?" Ben hooted. "Priceless. Wouldn't miss it for the world."

"You're not invited," I grumbled.

"Too bad. I'm coming anyway."

Ignoring him, I took my coffee back from Galloway and finished it. "Let's go. I'm keen to see what all the fuss is about this painting."

The Artistic Affair Art Gallery was surprisingly busy for a Sunday. I hadn't expected it to be open at all, but Abigail, the assistant manager, told us that weekends were their busiest time. Abigail was exactly what I expected an artsy person to be. Her hair was pitch black, piled on top of her head in a messy bun, her bangs cut so ultra-short that she reminded me of Suzi from the Tiger comic strip. She wore a tie-dye T-shirt knotted on one side, with striped cotton wide-legged pants and sequined ballet flats. Red glasses perched upon her nose, and her lips were painted a matching red. She looked fashionably on-trend, whereas I felt positively frumpy in comparison in my standard jeans and T-shirt.

She was tapping teal painted nails against her chin in response to Galloway's question about the painting. "You know, Keagan did bring a painting in for restoration," she said.

"Can we see it?" I asked.

"It's not here."

"Didn't you just say Keagan brought it in for restoration?" Galloway frowned.

She nodded. "He did. But then he took it. Maybe to his home studio? I don't really know. Paintings are his thing, I'm more into sculpture."

"Did you see the painting at all? Can you describe it?" Galloway asked. I opened my mouth to tell him I knew it was of a woman playing the piano but then clamped my lips shut, remembering what Ben had once advised. Let the subject you're interviewing tell the story, don't feed it to them.

"Oh, I can do one better. I snapped a photo of it." She glanced around as if afraid of being overheard and added in a hushed voice. "Don't tell Keagan. He was real protective of that painting, didn't want any of us going near it."

I glanced at Galloway, who returned my look with a raised brow. Odd that he'd be protective over an amateurish, worthless, painting. "He said he didn't want the public seeing it and thinking that was the standard of art we displayed here." Abigail continued. "He said it was a shame it was ever discovered, and it would be better to throw it straight in a skip rather than spend any time on it."

I felt the corners of my mouth turn down. For a minute there, I thought we might have been on to something, but it made sense. Keagan wanted to keep a certain standard of quality for his studio, he wouldn't want something of poor quality on display. Abigail pulled her phone out of her pants pocket, flicked through the screen, and then held it out to us.

Yep. A period painting of a woman playing the piano, another woman standing by the piano singing, and a man sitting enjoying the concert they were entertaining him with. I was a little puzzled. The painting didn't look too bad to me. The way everyone had been referring to it, I'd expected the scratching of a three-year-old.

"Could you send me a copy of that?" Galloway asked.

"Sure. I'll airdrop it." She glanced around. "Just...

don't tell Keagan, okay? As I said, he's real protective of it. He wouldn't like that I took a photo of it."

Ben, who'd taken a look at the picture on Abigail's phone, then disappeared through a door marked 'Studio—Private,' returned. "She's right. It's not here."

"Thank you." I smiled at Abigail, then followed Galloway out of the gallery. "What do you think?" I asked.

He shrugged. "I'm no art expert, but I'll see what we can find out about the painting." He glanced at his watch, then placed his hand on my lower back, guiding me to his car. "I got a message while we were talking to Abigail that the financials are in for the Finley's."

"Soooo... back to the station?"

"Nah. I can log in from your place. You can do your thing, and I'll mow the lawn." *Be still my beating heart!* Not only did he trust me to work the case with him, but he was prepared to do manual labor for me? I could hear my sister Laura's voice in my head. "He's a keeper!" I couldn't help but agree. Things were shaping up nicely with Captain Cowboy Hot Pants. My chest tightened, and I wasn't sure if it was the stirrings of love or utter panic. Yes, I had feelings for Galloway. Strong ones. And the stronger they got, the more terrified I felt. It was almost as if I were holding my breath, waiting for the other shoe to drop.

"If the wind changes, your face will be stuck like that." Ben elbowed me in the ribs. The cold blast jolted me back to awareness, and I quickly schooled my features, hurrying along behind Galloway grateful he hadn't seen the panic on my face.

Back home, I settled into the office, while Galloway headed outside, Thor and Ben hot on his heels. I was grateful for the distraction of not thinking about my future with Galloway and what it might hold. Or not.

The hours ticked by while I delved into the spreadsheets uploaded to the Firefly Bay Police Department servers. One thing was adding up, and it wasn't the numbers. I was frowning at the screen, tapping the pencil I'd been using to scribble notes when Galloway appeared in the doorway.

"I have no idea what your cat has been telling me," he said, "but it was a very long and apparently detailed story."

"Hmmm?" I glanced up, then back at the monitor before doing a double-take back at Galloway. He'd stripped off his shirt, and the glisten of sweat mixed with male pheromones had me practically drooling. Thor chose that moment to wind his way around Galloway's ankles before jumping up onto the corner of the desk.

"I was telling him about that time I got into a fight with the Persian at number fourteen," Thor said, accepting the head scratch I gave him with an appreciative purr. I relayed that nugget of information back to Galloway, who chuckled. "Well, I hope you won, Thor."

"Of course." Thor blinked, then yawned.

"How's it going with the accounts?" Galloway asked, pushing away from the doorframe where he'd been leaning and coming to stand behind me.

"Yeah, something's not right." I turned my attention back to the spreadsheet in front of me and dropped the pencil, using my finger to point at the entries. Thor immediately swatted the pencil onto the floor.

"These are all wrong."

"What am I looking at?" Galloway leaned closer, the heat of him hot against my back. Distracting. My pulse skittered, and I drew in a shaky breath, forcing myself to focus.

"This sheet is the supplier invoices for the last six months." I clicked to move to another tab on the spreadsheet. "And this one is the client invoices." I clicked once more. "And this is the overall transaction summary, combining incoming and outgoing."

"Right. And? You said something's not right?"

"Well, first of all, the formulas have been removed. When I go back, prior to six months, all of this was calculated with formulas, so the software was populating profit and loss and all of that automatically. But since here?" I tapped the screen. "It's manually calculated. And the figures are wrong. Not only that," I switched back to the supplier tab. "All of these supplier invoices have been overpaid. Only by a few dollars each, but it adds up."

"How do you know they've been overpaid?"

Navigating out of the spreadsheet, I opened up a folder that had hundreds of pdf files stored. "These are the originals. I thought I'd double-check a few, just to make sure, and then I've gone back over the past month. Every single invoice. Overpaid."

"How much are we talking here?"

"Over ten thousand in the past six months. And that's just my rough work — I haven't done a full audit, but as soon as I noticed the discrepancies, I started to make a note of it. You might want to get a forensic accountant to take a look, but..."

"Someone is stealing from Finley Construction," Galloway said grimly. I nodded. "And it could only be one person. His bookkeeper, Noreen Bellamy."

"Who is also one of our suspects."

"We know she had the opportunity. This gives us a motive." Had Anita caught Noreen stealing from the family business and confronted her about it? Anita hadn't said anything along those lines, but maybe she'd blocked it out? After all, being murdered was a traumatic experience. Ben had forgotten everything surrounding his death, and the cases he'd been working on. It had made finding his killer challenging, but not impossible.

Galloway's phone started to chime. Pulling it from

his back pocket, he hit the alarm button. "Time to get ready," he grinned.

"Get ready?"

"For dinner with your family."

"But what about Noreen? We need to go and question her!" I protested.

"It can wait until the morning. She's not going anywhere."

"But she might!" I argued. "What if she does a runner?"

"She's not aware that we're going through the financials. As far as she's concerned, she's gotten away with her skimming activities."

My face fell. I'd hoped we could confront Noreen this evening and get out of family dinner. Galloway, guessing where my mind had gone, chuckled and pulled me to my feet. "It's going to be fine."

"You don't know that." I pouted. It's not that my family is bad, far from it. It's just... the pressure. Both my brother and sister were happily married with offspring. I'm the only single one, and it felt like they were all waiting. Waiting for me to bring someone home. And for the first time ever, I was. Their expectations would be huge, and I was scared I'd cave under pressure and mess things up.

"I've got an idea that will take your mind off things," Galloway said. Before I could ask him what he scooped me over his shoulder in a fireman's hold, making me squeal, then swatted my butt as he carried me upstairs.

"What are you doing?" I panted, each step knocking the wind out of me.

"Shower." He replied smugly. We'd taken over the master suite purely for the luxurious bathroom. When I'd first moved into Ben's house, I'd slept in the guest room downstairs, the same room I'd always stayed in whenever I slept over. I couldn't bring myself to use the master suite, it was Ben's domain, and I hadn't been up to clearing out his personal belongings. Galloway had come to the rescue. He'd sent me out on a wild goose chase, and while I was gone, he'd packed up Ben's room. The clothes had gone to charity. Personal effects packed into boxes and put in storage. He'd even stripped the bed and bought all new bedding. I'd been incredibly touched and incredibly sad. If it wasn't for Ben himself telling me to get over myself, I'd probably still be using the guest room downstairs.

CHAPTER TEN

The tightness in my chest that had plagued me all day intensified, and for the life of me, I couldn't work out why. Taking a sip of wine, I watched Galloway manhandle my nieces and nephew, using them as weights as he lifted them in the air amidst squeals of laughter.

My sister Laura sidled up to me and nudged me with her elbow, a sly grin on her face. "Finally, caved, eh?"

I snorted. "Caved? The crafty witch went around me. Direct to the source."

Laura laughed. "Our mom can be determined."

"What do you mean, can be? She is bull-headed and stubborn."

"A lot like someone else I know." Brad, Laura's husband, joined us, sliding an arm around his wife's waist, his palm lingering against her abdomen in an intimate caress before settling on her hip. Then I noticed the clear liquid in Laura's glass. Not white wine. Water. Or straight vodka. Either was a possibility. I studied my sister's face, so similar to my own, then pointed a finger at her accusingly.

"You're glowing!"

A hint of color bloomed on her cheeks, and her mouth widened into a smile.

I dropped my voice to a harsh whisper. "Laura Nicholson... are you pregnant?"

Her grin was one of pure happiness, and the slight nod confirmed it. I squealed in delight then clapped a hand over my mouth. Throwing my arms around her neck, I hugged her tight. Brad rescued my wine glass before I tipped the contents down her back.

"We're announcing after dinner." She whispered in my ear. "Do you think you can keep our secret until then?"

I pulled back and eyeballed her. "Are you serious? Of course, I can."

My sister-in-law, Amanda, approached in her designer jeans and a silk button-down. Amanda was super-model gorgeous and, despite having a one-year-old and a three-year-old, was always impeccably dressed. "What's going on?" One perfectly arched brow lifted, her gaze going from me to Laura and back again.

"Nothing much." I shrugged. "Laura was just

wishing me well for my exam tomorrow." The lie fell smoothly from my lips, and I marveled at how easily I'd slipped into the role of secret keeper and stretcher of the truth.

"Is that tomorrow?" Amanda took a sip of her own wine. "That came around fast."

"Tell me about it," I sighed.

"So once you're fully qualified? Then what?"

"What do you mean?" I'd be a fully qualified private investigator. It wasn't rocket science.

She tilted her head toward Galloway, who was now rolling on the carpet with the children. "With him. He'll no longer be your supervisor. You won't be spending so much time together."

"I'm not sure what you're getting at?" Galloway and I didn't spend a lot of working hours together, despite him being my official supervisor while I underwent my PI training. We got together a couple of times a week to go over my cases, such as they were, and discuss general PI stuff like stake-outs and lately, firearms. I shuddered at the memory of my recent firearms lesson.

"How will you manage, Audrey, without him on a day-to-day basis?"

I stiffened, glanced at Laura, who was looking at Amanda with her mouth hanging open. Even Brad sported a frown, and he was the most easy-going guy around.

"Hold on." I straightened to my full five-foot-seven

height, which was still two inches shorter than Amanda. However, given the height of her stilettoes, I reckon we'd be on even footing if she ever took the damn things off. "Are you suggesting that Galloway is carrying me? That I'm not capable of being a PI?"

The funny thing about Amanda is that she mostly means well, it's just the way she says things that come out incredibly insulting. She saw my clumsiness as a huge disadvantage—for me—and was on an eternal quest to try to fix me. It chafed like leather pants on a summer's day.

"Yeah, Amanda!" Laura echoed, "just what are you insinuating here? That Audrey doesn't have what it takes? Because let me tell you, my little sister is ah-maz-ing. She is friggin epic! She is smart, she is brave, she is funny, and she is smart."

"You said smart," I whispered from the side of my mouth.

"I did?" She glanced at me.

"Yup." I nodded.

"Oh. Okay. Well, yeah, that still stands. She's doubly smart. And she doesn't need you or anyone else telling her otherwise."

"Hey, hey, hey!" Dustin, my brother and Amanda's husband, hurried over, no doubt sensing the climbing tension in the room. Hard to miss with both his sisters visibly bristling over yet another thoughtless comment from his wife. "What's going on over here?"

"Go ahead, Amanda." Laura snapped, "tell us what you meant. Because it sure didn't sound like you were wishing Audrey luck for her exam tomorrow!"

"Oh, that's right!" Dustin slapped a hand on my shoulder and squeezed. "Good luck for tomorrow. You'll ace it."

"Maybe you should tell your wife that," Laura said snidely, and I bit my lips to hide the grin. Hormonal Laura was fun.

"I'm sorry." Amanda apologized, sounding sincere. "That came out wrong." *Surprise, surprise.* "I wish you all the best on your exam tomorrow, Audrey."

"Thanks." Wait for it...

"It's just—"

"Babe." Dustin grabbed Amanda's elbow and steered her toward where Galloway was sitting cross-legged on the carpet, eyeing us while three toddlers climbed him like a jungle gym. "I'm pretty sure I can smell a dirty diaper."

Dustin's distraction technique worked. Amanda shoved her glass into his hand and scooped up Nathaniel, up-ending him and lifting his butt to her nose where she took a deep sniff, then screwed up her face. I expected her to palm her stinky offspring onto her husband; I mean come on, silk shirts and dirty diapers did not pair well. But to my utter shock, she tucked Nathaniel under one arm, scooped up the diaper bag from beside the sofa in her other hand, and disappeared down the hallway to take care of business.

"You know she means well," Dustin said apologetically, watching his wife.

"I know." I nodded. And I did. I hadn't really been sure what Amanda had been getting at, though. Did she think I couldn't manage the PI business on my own, that I didn't have the skills or smarts for it? Or did she mean now that Galloway wouldn't be my supervisor, our relationship would peter out? I hadn't missed the edge to her voice when she'd first brought up the subject.

Laura leaned in and whispered in my ear, "I think she's jealous."

I guffawed. "Of what? Me?"

"Why not? I meant everything I said. You're whip-smart, Audrey. And gorgeous. You have a beautiful house and your own business. You have a hot boyfriend. Girl, you've got it all going on."

"Uh, most of that just fell in my lap." I protested. "The house and business were Ben's, and if he hadn't died, I wouldn't be where I am today."

"True. But look at you, honoring his legacy, taking over his business—which I'm sure you'll be successful at."

Ben, who'd been hovering around my mom in the kitchen while she prepared her to die for lasagna, joined us. "I always liked your sister." He said, catching the tail end of Laura's speech. I ignored him. My family did not know of my ability to talk to ghosts, and I intended to keep it that way. Can you imagine if Amanda caught wind of it? She'd have me carted away by men in white coats before I could so much as blink. For my own good, of course.

"But also, I think she's a wee bit put out by your hot detective," Laura whispered, nudging me with her elbow, her eyes on Galloway, who was climbing to his feet, Isabelle, Laura's one-year-old balanced on his hip, while Dustin's three-year-old, Madeline, hitched a ride on his leg.

"Hey," Galloway handed Isabelle over to her father before his grey eyes landed on me, speculation in his gaze. "Need a drink?" He asked.

Laura barked out a laugh. "See? Perfect."

I smiled, ignoring my sister. "Yes, please." Brad had absconded with my glass, and I suspect he'd downed my drink behind his wife's back. Knowing Laura, if she had to be alcohol-free during her pregnancy, so did he. Galloway made his way to the kitchen where a bottle of wine sat open on the counter, Madeline still hanging from his leg, giggling as he took her for a ride.

"We heard the news about Anita Finley," Dustin said, filling the silence. "You involved in that case?" His question was directed at Galloway, who'd returned with my wine. After handing it over, he stayed close to my side, his warmth comforting.

"We are," Galloway said. "But we can't discuss the details, sorry. It's an active case."

"We?" Laura pounced. "Are you helping?" She asked me, and I nodded before taking a sip of wine. I was getting a nice little buzz happening, and I glanced toward the kitchen, hoping Mom served dinner soon; otherwise, there was a very strong chance I'd end up wasted before the night was through.

"Anita Finley was already my client," I said by way of explanation. "So yes, I'm helping the police with their inquiries."

"Actually, maybe you guys can help." Galloway surprised me by saying. Did he want their help? I thought we weren't meant to discuss the case. Now I was confused. He placed his hand at the small of my back as if to calm my turbulent thoughts. Or reassure me he knew what he was doing. Or maybe it was the fact that he couldn't keep his hands off me. I liked the latter theory the best.

"Anita was working at the Kelsh estate and found an artwork. I was wondering if any of you knew anything about art?" He removed his hand to reach for his phone, pulling up the photo the gallery assistant manager had given him.

"I know a little." Amanda had reappeared with Nathaniel on her hip. She tossed her long hair over her shoulder, freeing the strands from the toddler's chubby little fingers. "How can I help?"

"They found this painting at the Kelsh estate. Do you recognize it?" He held the phone up so everyone could see. Laura and Brad squinted at it and shook their heads. Dustin cocked his head. "It looks vaguely familiar." But Amanda? Amanda froze, the color draining from her face. She reached out a hand and took the phone from Galloway, pinching the screen with her fingers to enlarge the image.

"Oh, my God." She breathed.

"What? What is it?" Laura, and I said in unison.

Amanda looked up, shell-shocked. "Do you know what this is?" Her question was directed at Galloway.

"No. That's why I asked." He pointed out. "I'm guessing you recognize it?"

I looked from Galloway to Amanda and back again, holding my breath.

"I think this is... The Concert." She said it like we should all know what that meant. I had no clue. What was The Concert?

"What's that when it's at home?" Laura beat me to it.

"It's a famous painting by Johannes Vermeer, painted in sixteen sixty-four." She breathed, handing the phone back to Galloway. "It went missing in the nineties, stolen in a heist. No one has seen it since."

"You're saying it's valuable?" Galloway asked.

"Very." She handed her son over to Dustin and pulled out her own phone, fingers flying as she

Googled the painting. "Yes." She nodded. "It was stolen in nineteen ninety from the Isabella Stewart Gardner Museum in Boston."

"How much is it worth?" Brad asked.

"According to this article? Two hundred million."

"Holy cow!" I choked, looking up at Galloway. He met my look. There is no way Keagan Dunn, an art gallery owner, did not know the painting was the real deal. Yet he'd lied, to everyone, about its value. That gave him not only the opportunity but motive. A massive motive. Two hundred million dollars' worth of motive. I turned, searching for somewhere to put down my drink. Galloway wrapped his fingers around my wrist, halting me before lowering his lips to my ear. "We are not tearing out of here to go question him." His breath blew hot against my skin, and I moistened my lips with my tongue to keep from swooning. "It can wait till tomorrow."

I looked up at him from beneath my lashes. "You're sure?"

"Positive." He lifted his head and directed his next words to Amanda. "Thanks for that, you were very helpful." Amanda preened at the praise, bestowing him with a proud smile.

"Dinner's ready!" Mom called. That settled it. We definitely weren't going anywhere until after dinner, no way was I going to miss mom's lasagna.

CHAPTER ELEVEN

Holding my T-shirt away from my body, I tugged until the fabric reached the flowing faucet, scrubbing at the glob of orange sauce. I hadn't missed Amanda's rolled eyes when I'd dropped a forkful of Lasagna down my front. I'd warned Galloway this would most likely happen, and he'd looked at me with the most gorgeous smile, eyes sparkling, had cupped my nape, and leaned in real close to say, "You think I don't know that about you by now, Fitz." And winked before dropping a kiss on the tip of my nose.

The entire table had gone silent, watching our exchange. I'd heard both Laura and my mom sigh. Ben, who'd been sitting on the kitchen bench next to the dining room, guffawed. "He's sealed the deal now, Fitz. Your family loves him." I wanted to reply, "of course they do!" but instead allowed my own smile to bloom and finally, finally, let myself relax.

"All good in here?" Laura poked her head into the bathroom, where I was attempting to get the worse of the stain out. I looked down at myself, at my now distinctly wet T-shirt and the orange smear I'd spread across the fabric. I grinned at my sister. "I think I got it all."

"Nailed it." She winked, and we both laughed. She leaned into the bathroom a little further. "Are you almost finished, though?"

"Oh! Your announcement!" Turning off the faucet, I squeezed as much water as I could out of my shirt, dried my hands on a towel, and ignored the wet, clammy sensation against my stomach and chest as the wet patch slowly spread. "Let's do this." Linking my arm with hers, we returned to the dining room.

Amanda's eyes zoomed in on the mess I'd made of my shirt, but when she opened her mouth to comment, Dustin elbowed her in the ribs. Her mouth closed with a snap, and I shot my brother a grateful look.

Brad stood when his wife approached, and I quickly took my seat next to Galloway, squeezing his thigh under the table. He dropped his hand over mine, and we looked toward Brad and Laura, who stood with their arms around each other's waists and addressed the table.

"We're pregnant!" Laura blurted without preamble.

There was a moment's silence, then all hell broke loose. Mom cried, practically tipping her chair over to get to Laura and envelope her in a hug. There were hugs, tears, handshakes, and toasts, and it was wonderful. I couldn't be happier for my sister, she and Brad deserved all the happiness in the world. And, on a more selfish note, it took the attention away from Galloway and me, my tension eased so much so that when Galloway grabbed my arm and dragged me away to a quiet corner, I was unprepared for what he had to say.

"I've gotta go."

"What?" I reared back, eyes scouring his face. Had all this talk of babies freaked him out? Oh the irony, just as I'd relaxed, he'd tensed up.

He showed me his phone, but I couldn't make out the stream of messages on the screen. "I put in for a search warrant of Keagan's home and the gallery." He told me, keeping his voice low so the others wouldn't overhear us. "It's just come through."

"I thought you said it could wait?" Then the penny dropped, and I gasped, clutching my throat. "Kade Galloway, did you lie to me?"

He smirked, an adorable tilting of his upper lip. "Guilty as charged. You can punish me later."

"Oh, I intend to." I glanced over my shoulder at my family, who was gathered around Laura and Brad. "I'm coming with you."

"You can't be involved in the search." He pointed out.

"That's fine. I'll wait in the car. But you're not leaving me here on my own. As soon as you're gone, the attention will turn from Laura and Brad to you and me, and I am so not in the mood for the third degree. Mom is all babies and happily ever after right now."

"And that's a bad thing?" He quirked one brow, and I marveled at how he could individually control his eyebrows like that. Whenever I attempted it, both of my eyebrows either shot into my hairline or furrowed so deep and low I could barely see. Not to mention my mouth and nose joined in the facial workout. I know this because I've spent way too long in front of a mirror practicing.

"It's a timing thing." I skirted around the subject. "Let Brad and Laura have their moment."

"Okay. But you have to stay in the car." Almost giddy with delight that he'd agreed, we made our goodbyes and high-tailed it out of there.

"What's up?" Ben asked, joining us.

"Galloway has a search warrant for Keagan's place," I explained as we drove all of ten minutes to Keagan Dunn's house.

"Smart." Ben nodded, leaning in between the front seats.

"And fast," I added, hinting that Galloway needed to spill.

He threw a glance my way while pulling into Keagan's driveway. "I knew it would take time to get the warrant. Especially on a Sunday night, it's doubtful the judge is happy we interrupted his evening. I didn't want you to get yourself worked up when you were meant to be enjoying time with your family, so yeah, I kept it to myself."

"But we're here now, executing the warrant. Not in the morning, like you'd told me. You think he's a flight risk?"

"I think he knows he has a two hundred-million-dollar painting in his possession. I also think he has a way he can move that painting, sell it to a collector, without ever getting found out. But now we're sniffing around. No doubt his assistant manager told him we were in his gallery this morning. What would your next steps be if you were him?"

"Get the hell out of Dodge. Or at least get rid of the incriminating evidence."

"Exactly." We both looked through the windshield at Keagan's house. Almost every light was on, pools of light bursting through gaps in the curtains and blinds.

"He's packing."

Galloway nodded. "I'd say so."

"Sooooo..." I looked at him. "What are you waiting for?"

"Backup. And the warrant." Just as he said the words, a patrol car pulled in behind us. Galloway opened his door, but before he got out, he turned back to me. "Stay in the car."

"I know, I know," I grumbled, crossing my arms over my chest and doing my best not to pout.

Ben laughed and patted my shoulder. "Don't worry, Fitz. I'll report back to you." I scowled, even more put out that my ghost friend could go where I could not.

Galloway closed the door, and I turned in my seat to watch him walk back to the patrol car. Officer Noah Walsh was in the driver's seat, Sergeant Addison Young in the passenger seat, warrant in hand. I watched as they climbed out of the car, conversed with Galloway for a minute before approaching the front door. Young banged on the door with her fist. "Firefly Bay PD. Open up." She yelled.

I watched while Ben walked around the officers and straight through the front door, seconds later sticking his head back through it and calling out to me, "he's making a run for it—back door."

Unable to wind down my window since Galloway had taken the keys, and the windows were electric, I opened the door. Galloway swiveled and glared at me. I jerked my head toward the side gate and mouthed "out the back," hoping he'd understand that we had some spiritual help. He cocked his head for a second, then realization dawned.

"Bust it down." He ordered. "I'll take the back." He drew his weapon from the back of his jeans, and darted down the side of the house, vaulting over the gate as if it were nothing. Walsh kicked in the front door, and he and Young stormed inside, weapons drawn, yelling for Keagan and identifying themselves as Police. I sat in the passenger seat, my attention divided between the front of the house where Young and Walsh had just disappeared, and the pathway leading to the rear where the darkness had swallowed Galloway mere seconds ago.

Minutes ticked by. Minutes that felt like hours. I was on the edge of my seat, peering through the windshield, bursting with curiosity. But I made myself stay put. This was an official police warrant. If I got involved, it could jeopardize the entire case. I knew that. But I didn't like it.

Imagine my surprise when the garage door directly in front of Galloway's car opened. Ducking low, I peered over the dash. Keagan had evaded Galloway and got into his garage. I figured Galloway and the others would hear the garage door as it swung upward, but no-one appeared, and I feared Keagan actually had a shot at getting away.

Timing was everything. Screwing my eyes tightly closed, I held my breath and listened, heard the pounding of his footsteps as he neared Galloway's car, and just as he drew level with my door, I swung it open. Hard. There was that satisfying clunk as Keagan ran straight into it, then the oof as he landed on his back on the ground. I sprang out of the car, flipped him onto his stomach, and sat on him.

"Galloway!" I yelled.

"Audrey? What the hell?" Galloway came running, skidding to a halt when he saw me perched on Keagan's back. "You okay?"

"I'm fine. Sorry. I know you said to stay in the car, but I couldn't let him get away."

Walsh and Young appeared, then sniggered when they saw me sitting on their perp. "Nice." Walsh grinned, before stepping forward with his cuffs. "Thanks, Audrey, we'll take it from here."

I hauled myself off of Keagan, stumbling and almost falling flat on my face before catching myself and getting my feet under me. I turned and grinned at Galloway, who, I was pretty sure, was biting back a smile. Maybe. I cocked my head, considering his stony visage. He couldn't be mad, *could he?* I'd stopped Keagan from getting away.

"What happens now? Is he under arrest?" I ignored Galloway and turned my attention to Walsh as he bundled Keagan into the back of the patrol car.

"Depends on what we find in the house," Young said, hands on hips. "Walsh, keep an eye on him. You okay to assist me with the search warrant?" She asked Galloway.

"Certainly." He replied, looking at me and jerking his thumb toward his car.

"I know, I know, I'll wait in the car." I huffed, traipsing back to the vehicle. I paused to peer at the passenger door, wondering if Keagan had dented it.

"Fitz?" Galloway stopped me. "Good job."

I beamed, but before I could say anything, he continued on. "All the best detective's have one thing in common—"

"Plucky sidekick?"

"Besides that." He deadpanned.

"Ethics?" I tried again.

"Besides that."

"I give up. What?"

"Initiative." With that, he spun on his heel and followed Sergeant Young inside the house.

"I don't get it," I muttered under my breath as I climbed into the passenger seat and shut the door. Was he mad at me or pleased with me?

"He meant it as a compliment," Ben said. I let out a startled shriek then clapped my hand over my mouth, swiveling to look out the back windshield to see Officer Walsh glance my way, but he stayed by the side of the patrol car, arms crossed over his chest while he waited for Galloway and Young to search the house.

Lowering my voice, I whispered, "how so?"

"You followed instructions—stay in the car—yet you effectively stopped Dunn from escaping without putting yourself at risk."

I shrugged. "Yeah, but I..." I trailed off.

"Did it without thinking?" Ben offered. "Did it instinctively? Used your intuition?"

"Ooooooh." I got it now.

"Intuition is like common sense." Ben moved from the rear seat to the driver's seat. "Not everyone has it."

"Roger that." I'd discovered that to be true from my years as an office temp. As a person who had common sense, it had come as a shock to discover not everyone was blessed with the trait.

Flashing lights caught my attention, and I adjusted the rearview to see another patrol car roll up. Officer's Jacobs and Collier climbed out, stopped for a brief word with Walsh, before heading on up to Keagan's house. Had they found something? The painting, perhaps?

An hour dragged by. My eyelids were drooping, and I smothered a yawn. My bladder was telling me sitting and waiting in Galloway's car for much longer was not an option. Not if he didn't want damp upholstery. Just as I was considering my options, the driver's side door opened, and he climbed in. Ben moved out of the way just in time, retreating to his spot in the back.

"All done?" I yawned.

"The crew is just wrapping up." Galloway nodded. "Sorry I kept you waiting out here. I should have gotten someone to drop you home."

"That's okay," I lied. "I got in some swatting for my

exam." It was true. Ben had quizzed me to within an inch of my life. So much so that my brain hurt.

"Damn, I forgot you had your exam tomorrow." He glanced at his watch and winced. "Geez, sorry Audrey, I should have given you the keys so you could take yourself home."

"Coulda, shoulda, woulda." I lifted a shoulder. "But if you're done now, can we go? I need the bathroom."

"Oh, man. I messed up on this one, huh?" He started the engine. The patrol car that had been behind us had left twenty minutes ago, taking Keagan to the station. If I'd thought of it, I could have hitched a ride with them, pretty sure Walsh would have been okay with dropping me home.

"I take it you found the painting?" Crossing my legs, I concentrated on my pelvic floor muscles as every little bump in the road added extra pressure to my bladder.

"And then some!" Galloway snorted, shooting me a glance before turning his attention back to the road. "It looks like Dunn has himself a nice little counterfeit setup going on."

"Counterfeit?" I frowned. "As in money?"

"As in paintings." Galloway corrected. "His home studio was full of the same painting. Complete with the forged artist's signature. That's what took so long. We had to confirm they were rip-offs, that he wasn't copying his own work—which isn't illegal."

"But did you find the painting? The Concert one?" The one worth two hundred million dollars. I couldn't comprehend that amount of money. While I'd been waiting, I'd puzzled over why it had been in the attic of Dudley Kelsh's farmhouse, of all places. So far, the only theory I'd come up with was that Dudley Kelsh had been a thief. What didn't make sense was why he hadn't sold the stolen painting? Why live in a run-down old farmhouse when you have a painting worth millions at your disposal?

"Sure did." Galloway grinned, reaching out and squeezing my knee. "Thanks to your sister-in-law."

"Yay." I raised my fist in a lackluster cheer. *Go, Amanda.*

"This is going to attract a lot of media attention."

"Right."

"I'm going to be tied up at the station for a while."

"That's okay." I didn't expect anything less. We'd pulled up outside my place, and Galloway kept the engine idling. "Oh. Right. Drop and roll." I opened my door, preparing to leave.

"Sorry." His eyes pleaded with me to understand. It rankled that he felt the need to apologize, and I turned back to face him, eyes blazing. "Don't ever apologize for doing your job."

He reared back, not so much at my words, but I suspect the delivery. I sucked in a breath and slowly released it. "I'm not mad. Honest. But... I do need to pee, so I can't stand here chit-chatting with you. And you have an art thief to go interrogate."

"If I don't see you before, good luck with your exam tomorrow!"

I waved thanks and slammed the door shut, hurrying up to my front door, keys already in hand. I hadn't been lying when I said I needed to pee. The house was dark, and I flipped on the lights, punched in the code on the alarm, then hurried to the bathroom. Through the door, I could hear Ben talking with Thor and smiled.

"Now what?" Ben asked as soon as I finished in the bathroom, while Thor was the usual, "my food bowl is empty."

Scooping Thor up into my arms, I snuggled my face into his fur, enjoying the rumble of his purr as I carried him to his food bowl, which was most assuredly, not empty. Putting him on the floor, I rearranged the kibble into a neat pile and chuckled when he pushed my hand out of the way to scoff down the crunchy treats.

"Right," I said to Ben, dusting off my hands. "We've got work to do."

"Right on!" Ben bounced from one foot to the other, hyped. "What are you thinking? That Keagan killed Anita because of the painting? Maybe she suspected something was up?"

"No." I chewed on a nail, thinking. "It doesn't make

sense." Hightailing it to the whiteboard in my office, I picked up a marker and wrote Anita's name on the board. Ben leaned back against the desk and watched.

"Anita's food was spiked, which tells me her death was premeditated. It took planning. And there were no guarantees Anita would even eat the contaminated noodle cup. And if she did, when. It could have been a couple of days before she got to the contaminated one, if at all."

"That doesn't mean Keagan couldn't have done it."

"True, but again, why? We already know from Anita herself that she had no clue the painting was valuable. And while I didn't get a look at Keagan's home studio, I wouldn't be surprised if he'd made a copy of the original painting, a knock off he could give back to Anita so she could hang it at the museum or historical society. He didn't need to kill her to keep her off his back."

"You're saying Keagan Dunn is guilty of art fraud and possession of stolen goods, but not murder."

"Yes." I turned my attention back to the whiteboard and wrote Noreen Bellamy's name. "I think Noreen's been cooking the books. I got access to Finley Construction accounts, and it looks to me like she's been embezzling."

"Can you prove it was her? Maybe it was Logan? Or even Tyler."

"Noreen is Logan's bookkeeper."

"That doesn't make her guilty."

I rolled my eyes. "Now you're just being argumentative." I put a question mark beneath Noreen's name. "Finley Constructions isn't her only client. She's also the treasurer for the historical society."

"You think she's embezzling from them too?"

"From what I can tell, the money started going missing from Logan's account six months ago, small amounts spread out over numerous transactions. What's to say she hasn't been doing that with all her clients? A few hundred here, a few hundred there?"

"But Noreen doesn't appear to have been on any big spending sprees. No flashy clothes, no fancy car."

"That we've seen. Maybe Anita asked to see the books for the society, and Noreen panicked and killed her."

"It's possible." Ben conceded.

"Keagan and Noreen were at the museum that morning. She could have ducked into the society and laced the noodle cup."

"So could Keagan." Ben pointed out.

I wrinkled my nose. "Basically, our two suspects are each other's alibi." I snapped my fingers. "Maybe they're in it together?"

"Doubtful. What would Keagan need with a few thousand dollars embezzled from Noreen's clients when he had a painting worth a fortune in his possession?

One he knew he could shift on the black market, judging by the counterfeit setup he had going on at his house."

"You're right." I stepped back and surveyed the whiteboard. Two names. Both with motive and opportunity.

"The way Anita was killed," Ben moved into my line of sight to stare at the board, "leans more towards a female killer than a male. Women tend to adopt the poison method."

"But she wasn't poisoned. Although lacing her food with the one thing she is deadly allergic to is as good as." I nodded. "Fair point. Plus, I'm not liking Keagan for this. If he's into black-market arts goods and nefarious schemes, he'd probably have shot her if she became a problem. Or got someone else to."

"Agreed."

I put a line through Keagan's name. He was not our killer.

"Which leaves Noreen. I want to get a look at the society's books. Noreen doesn't know the police got a warrant for Finley's finances, so she doesn't know we know what she's been doing."

"What about Logan?" Ben asked.

"What about him?"

"He's not on the board." He cocked his head at the whiteboard in front of us.

"You think he should be?"

"Anita said it herself that he'd been acting strangely. Secretive."

"Yes, but I think I know why." I tapped Noreen's name. "His business was in trouble. He started Finley Constructions twenty-two years ago, he's a proud man who didn't want to bother his wife with the fact that he owed contractors and suppliers money he doesn't have. Money that Noreen stole."

"You're assuming that's what had him acting strangely." Ben crossed his arms and frowned at me. "Anita told me she has a life insurance policy. That money would bail him out of his financial troubles."

I sucked in a breath through my teeth. "True," I added his name to the board.

"Something else is puzzling me." I tapped the whiteboard with the marker. "The missing EpiPen. And the necklace."

"I can't believe you're still caught up on that necklace." Ben groaned.

"Because it's a mystery! It's what Anita hired me for. It has to be involved with all of this, I do not buy that it just disappeared all on its own. And we have Anita's own account—she didn't wear it. She got it out ready to wear but never took it out of the box. Next thing you know, the box and necklace are gone."

I yawned, the whiteboard blurring as I studied the names.

"You look beat," Ben said. "And it's late. Why not get some rest and start afresh in the morning?"

He was right. I couldn't do anything about the historical society's books tonight, and Galloway would be tied up at the station for hours. Time for some shuteye, finding the killer would have to wait until tomorrow.

CHAPTER TWELVE

Because I spent the weekend hunting a killer and not grocery shopping as I'd intended, my cupboards were bare come Monday morning. Which is why I found myself at the Firefly Bay Hotel for breakfast. And, I admit, there are plenty of choices when it came to dining out in Firefly Bay. Still, I had another reason for currently sitting in their restaurant waiting for my Spanish omelet. Lacey Stevens.

It had come to me last night as I was dozing off. Lacey Stevens and her odd behavior. She hadn't turned up for cleaning duty at the museum Saturday morning, she'd hung around to eavesdrop later on at the Finley's house. Despite only living in Firefly Bay for a few months, in that time she'd become Anita's

BFF and had insinuated herself very comfortably into Anita's life.

Not that any of that was wrong. Or made her a killer. But I was curious. Taking a sip of the amazingly good cup of coffee the waitress had delivered I pulled out my phone and pretended I was on a call so that I could talk to Ben who was sitting opposite me, or rather, hovering in the middle of the table because the chair wasn't pulled out.

"After this, I'm heading to the historical society to look at their accounts," I said into the phone.

"I know Galloway asked you to consult on the accounting thing, specifically the warrant for the Finley accounts. Does it extend to the historical society?"

"No. But that's not going to stop me. I just need a quick look. If my suspicions are correct," I paused and glanced around, making sure no one could overhear me, "then Noreen is our money thief."

"And if the books aren't cooked?"

I frowned. I'd thought of that too and hadn't liked the answer. "Then suspicion is back on Logan. Or Tyler. I just don't understand why Logan would steal from himself. If he needed money from the business, he could just take it, he didn't need to hide it."

"That theory then lends itself to Tyler who's doing the skimming." Ben pointed out.

I sighed. "I know." It wasn't a scenario I relished,

but if I could clear Noreen, then it was Tyler I'd be looking at next.

"Speaking of..." Ben pointed across the dining room, and I turned my head to look. There stood Lacey and Tyler, arguing.

"Go over there!" I hissed. "Find out what that's all about."

Putting my phone down on the table, I watched with burning curiosity. Tyler's hands were clenched into fists as if angry, yet his face was a picture of anguish. Lacey seemed indifferent, her hand signals cutting him off. She clearly wasn't interested in what he had to say. As if sensing me watching, her head snapped around, and our eyes collided. She stared me down for a few seconds before turning her attention back to Tyler.

Whatever she said crushed him. His shoulders slumped like a deflated balloon, and his chin lowered to his chest. Lacey spun on her heel and disappeared into the kitchen. Tyler shuffled toward the front doors, head down, not noticing anything around him. Ben returned, and I picked up my phone again.

"Well?" I prompted.

"He was saying something about her giving it back. And that he shouldn't have given it to her in the first place, it was a mistake."

"What did she say?"

"She said it wasn't going to happen, and he needed to get over himself."

"He seemed really upset."

"He was. I thought he was going to cry... but... get this. He issued her some sort of ultimatum. To return whatever it was, or they were through."

"Through?" I pounced on the word. "As in? They're having a relationship?" I blanched. Lacey was old enough to be his mom!

"It looked and sounded that way." Ben nodded.

"And what did Lacey say about that? The ultimatum?"

"She said, whatever, and walked away."

Through the front windows of the restaurant, I caught sight of Tyler, climbing into the Finley Constructions truck. Slamming his fist on the steering wheel, he glared out the windshield before starting the engine and roaring off, tires squealing.

"What if..." I played with the salt shaker on the table, spinning it until it fell over, and salt spilled onto the tablecloth. Hastily I righted it. "What if the thing that Tyler wants back is his mom's necklace?"

"Not a silly suggestion." Ben nodded. Spotting the waitress heading my way with my omelet, he moved aside. "I'm going to find Anita, see what we can dig up. And Audrey? Don't forget to set an alarm for your exam."

Shoot. I grabbed my phone and dutifully set an

alarm. It helped that I had a case to work on keeping my nerves at bay, but the downside of having a case to work on was that I'd get so involved in it I'd lose track of time. My exam was at two, at the Council offices. If I missed it, I'd have to pay the fee all over again, not to mention re-schedule.

"Thank you." I smiled at the waitress as she slid a steaming plate in front of me.

"Is there anything else I can help you with today?" She asked.

"No, thanks. I'm good." I smiled again and waited until she walked away before picking up my cutlery and digging in. Mmmmm. Delicious. My eyes rolled in my head as the cheesy goodness melted on my tongue. This was exactly what I needed. Refuel with a good meal, excellent coffee, then it was time to dig the dirt on Noreen Bellamy.

I lingered at the restaurant for another cup of coffee, hoping to catch a glimpse of Lacey, quiz her on her relationship with Tyler, but she remained in the kitchen, even when I sent word via the waitress of "my compliments to the chef."

Unable to dawdle any longer, I left a tip and hurried out to my car, just in time to take a call from my mom. Connecting it to Bluetooth, I answered as I drove.

"Hi, Mom, what's up?" I figured she was calling to gossip about Laura and Brad and the baby.

"Kade is on the news." She surprised me by saying.

"He is?"

"Yes. They're saying that Keagan Dunn, the chap who owns that boutique art gallery next door to the museum, has been arrested for art fraud and receiving stolen goods."

"Ah, yeah. That." Galloway had warned me that the media would be all over it, I just hadn't expected the news to hit so soon.

"You knew?" Mom squawked.

"Yes, I did. But I can't talk about it, Mom." I warned her. "It's a police investigation, not a PI thing."

"Okay fine." She huffed. Then, "last night went well, didn't it? And fantastic news about the baby!"

The next five minutes were spent listening to Mom plan out the baby's arrival, baby-sitting duties for Isabelle when Laura went into labor, and what they'd need for the nursery. Pulling into the parking lot of the historical society, I parked beneath a tree.

"Mom, Laura's got months to go before the baby arrives. There's plenty of time."

"I know, love. It's just exciting."

I smiled. "You're right. It is. Look, Mom, I've arrived at where I need to be, so I've gotta go."

"Good luck with your exam today, love, I'll be thinking of you. Love you."

"Love you too, Mom. And thanks. Bye."

Retrieving my phone from its cradle, I hung up

then surveyed the lot. No cars other than my own, and one canary yellow mobility scooter was parked near the front door of the combined historical society slash museum. I was reasonably sure Noreen drove a Honda Civic, white, of which there was no sign.

The front door to the society was unlocked, so I pushed it open and stepped inside. Like Saturday morning, it was chilly and smelled somewhat stale, but I could hear a radio playing, so I followed the sound until I found Mary Wilson, the society's secretary, in a tiny office not dissimilar to Anita's.

"Hey," I knocked on the open door, and she gasped. "Sorry, didn't mean to startle you." I smiled by way of apology.

She returned the smile and turned the radio down. "Sorry, I like to play it loud when I'm here alone—it can get a little spooky."

I nodded. "I bet."

"Audrey, isn't it? You were here Friday night? Anita said something about helping with the Kelsh estate?" Before I could respond, she continued. "What terrible news about Anita! Dead! It's just awful. I can't imagine what the society will do without her. And then there's this business with Keagan." Her brows pulled low, as did her voice. "Whatever was he up to? Art fraud the news said. And receiving stolen goods. I wonder what that was all about?"

"I—"

"I'm getting ready to call an emergency meeting. With the president and vice-president roles both empty, we need to fill those positions ASAP."

I bit my lip to stop myself from telling her they may need a new treasurer as well.

"Are you interested in the position, Mary?" I asked instead.

"Who me?" Her hand fluttered to her neck, fingers playing with the gold cross hanging there. "Well." She cleared her throat. "If the rest of the committee nominates me, I guess I could consider it."

"I'm sure you'd make a wonderful president." I smiled. "So, I, uh, dropped in to see if it was okay if I took a look at where Anita was up to with the Kelsh estate? Since we didn't get to work on it together because she... you know..."

"Oh! Of course! I'm sure that will be fine. Follow me." She bustled out of her office as fast as her arthritic knees would allow, and I fell into step beside her. I thought we were going to Anita's office, but she stopped before we reached it and unlocked a different door. Swinging it open, she pointed at a windowless room housing one table, one chair, and a computer.

"This is our IT room." She declared with dramatic flair. "We only have one computer, and since everyone wanted access to it, we decided it was best if it had its own office."

"Right." I nodded. "No network, then?"

"No budget." She sniffed. "Anita was working towards us getting our own server and each having our own networked computers, but alas, the bank balance seemed to be continually falling, despite Anita's fundraising efforts."

Flicking on the light, Mary ushered me inside. "Password is History and number one. I don't know much about Anita's files on the Kelsh estate, but there's a folder on the desktop marked President. I suggest you look in there."

"Thanks, Mary. I won't be long, I'll just print out where Anita was up to with the cataloging, and then I'll be out of your hair."

"Take your time, love. Noreen won't be in for another hour, she does the accounts every Monday morning."

"She does the accounts here? Not from home?"

"She says it gets her out of the house, coming here. It helps me out as well since she picks up the mail on the way."

Good to know. "The computer will be free by then," I assured her before pulling out the chair and sitting down. I waited until she'd shuffled off down the hallway before turning the computer on. While it was booting up, I pulled an empty USB out of my bag and sat it by the keyboard. One thing I knew about Noreen Bellamy was she liked to use spreadsheets over an accounting software package, which made what I had to do that much easier.

Just like Mary had told me, there was a folder on the desktop with each of the member's positions. Shoving the USB in, I copied the entire contents of Anita's folder, then opened Noreen's treasurer folder. Inside the main folder was a bunch of sub-folders sorted by year. I copied the entire contents of the current year over to the storage device.

While the computer was busy copying all the files, I opened Anita's folder and copied the contents over to the USB drive as well, before searching for the Kelsh estate file. As predicted, Anita had a spreadsheet on the contents of the Kelsh estate, her attempt at cataloging, and I opened it up and hit print. Mary didn't need to know I'd copied all the files I needed. Since the Kelsh catalog was the only one I'd opened, anyone using the computer after me, aka Noreen, wouldn't know I'd been in her files.

As soon as the USB stopped flashing, I ejected it and dropped it in my bag, then shut the computer down and scooped up the spreadsheet from the printer.

"All done, Mary!" I stopped in the doorway of Mary's office and waved the printout at her. "Thank you."

"That's okay, love. Thank you for helping. The society appreciates it. I don't suppose you're interested in joining the committee? We have a couple of vacancies."

"I'll think about it." I lied, giving her a wave and heading off down the hallway. Once I've found Anita's killer and closed the case, my work with the society will be done.

CHAPTER THIRTEEN

ack home, I stood in front of the whiteboard and added Lacey Stevens as a suspect. "There's more to you than meets the eye."

"Who me?" Thor yawned from his position on the corner of the desk.

"No. Her." I pointed to Lacey's name. "Ben and I think she may be having an affair with Anita's son." Urgh, even saying the words out loud felt wrong. "And if that's true, then she has a possible motive. And opportunity." I recalled Anita telling me that as she'd driven away from the museum on Friday night, Lacey had stopped to take a call. She could easily have let herself back into the building and laced the noodle cup. "But why kill Anita?" I muttered to myself. "You came to town six months ago, became instant best friends with Anita... was that to get to her son? Was it all some sort of ruse?" I had more questions than I had answers.

Thor laid down on the keyboard. "Riveting. Wake me up when it's lunchtime."

Scooping him up from the keyboard, I deposited him on the floor. "I need that, champ." I had the historical society's accounts to go over. Not to mention Anita's files I'd taken on a whim. They may reveal something of interest.

Sad to say it didn't take me long to discover discrepancies in the society's accounts. Similar to the Finley accounts, invoices had been overpaid. Not by much, but a little here and there soon adds up. What I didn't have was the account number the extra funds were being diverted to. I'd need police assistance to access Noreen's bank accounts, or I needed to confront the woman herself. But there was no doubt in my mind that Noreen Bellamy was stealing from her clients. Whether she'd killed Anita because of it was another matter.

I put a call into Galloway. When he didn't pick up, I left a message asking him to call me back, then snatched up my keys and headed back to the historical society, hoping to catch Noreen there.

"Oh, sorry, love. You just missed her. She's gone home for lunch, and then she's off to Finley Constructions." Mary told me, busy going through the pile of mail Noreen had brought with her. "You should have said you wanted to talk to her, and I would have passed on a message."

"Really? She's going into Finley Constructions today?" I considered Mary, who was looking a little flushed as she busied herself with the mail, and somewhere along the way, she'd lost an earring.

"I have to admit I was a little surprised too. But she said she had some work to finish."

"Thanks, Mary, I'll try to catch her at home. She's still on...?"

"Kloeden Lane. Third on the right, can't miss it, has a yellow door."

"Thanks." With a wave, I hurried back to my car.

Noreen was not at home, so I figured I'd find her at Finley Constructions. Thankfully, in the town the size of Firefly Bay, it only took mere minutes to get anywhere, so in seven minutes and twenty seconds, I was pulling into a construction yard on Turner Avenue. A high chain-link fence surrounded the property, but the two gates stood open, a chain with padlock dangling from one of them. Lumber was stacked inside a massive shed to my left, only the front of the shed was open, allowing easy access for the truck and forklift parked beside it. At the rear of the property, I could see mounds of what appeared to be gravel and sand and to my right, a shipping container that had been turned into an office.

I knew this because it had a sign that said *office*

hanging over the door. Parked beside the office was a white Honda Civic. Stopping beside it, I climbed out and approached, rapping my knuckles on the door as I opened it and stepped inside.

"Audrey?"

I blinked toward Noreen's voice, my eyes adjusting from the brightness outside to the dim light in the office. "Hi, Noreen." Blink. I could just make out her silhouette, and furniture was beginning to take shape. Once my vision had adjusted, I took a good look around. Logan had done a wonderful job of converting the shipping container. From inside, I wouldn't have known at all. A desk sat at each end of the room, and behind one of them sat Noreen.

"What are you doing here?" she asked.

"How long have you been embezzling from your clients?" I blurted.

Noreen blanched, the color draining from her face. "What?" She squeaked.

"You heard me." I crossed my arms over my chest. "You've been stealing from Finley Constructions and the historical society. And I bet if I were to take a look at the accounts of your other clients, I'd find some interesting anomalies there too."

Noreen busied herself with moving items around her desk. First, a calculator, from her left to her right, then a notebook which she closed, then opened again.

She picked up a pencil, fumbled with it until it slipped from her fingers to clatter on the desk.

"Is that why you killed Anita?" I asked when it seemed she wasn't going to respond. "She found out, and you had to silence her?"

"What! No. No, I didn't hurt Anita, there's no way I'd do anything to harm her!" Noreen protested, finally meeting my eyes.

"Soooo, stealing from her isn't hurting her?"

She lifted one shoulder. "It wasn't much. They could afford it."

"And that makes it okay?"

Lowering her chin to her chest, she whispered, "I'm sorry."

"Why? What made you decide to steal from the people who trusted you to look after their money? And the historical society? It's a not-for-profit organization, how could you steal from them?"

"I wanted to go on a cruise." She whispered.

I blinked in shock. "A cruise?"

"Yes. A single's cruise. I'm fifty years old and have never been married. It's been years since I've even had a boyfriend. Even longer since I've had a holiday. Caring for Mom has been a financial drain. And then one night, I saw this ad for a mature age single's cruise, and it was perfect!" Her voice became as animated as her hands as she started waving them around, describing the cruise she was prepared to steal for. "Sixteen nights. It departs Fort Lauderdale, and then we go to Jamaica, Costa Rica, Panama, Guatemala, Mexico, and San Francisco."

"And how much was this cruise?"

"Three and a half thousand dollars."

I cocked my head. "But you've stolen over ten thousand from the Finley's alone. More than enough to pay for the cruise. Why keep stealing?"

She dropped her head. "It was just... easy. Incredibly easy. No one even noticed, so I just... kept on doing it."

"And where is the money now?"

"In my bank account. I can give it back. I *will* give it back. Just don't call the police. Please!"

"Sorry, Noreen. They already know." Well, not for sure, not one hundred percent confirmed, but as soon as Galloway called me back, then they'd know.

She flopped back in her chair. "Are they coming? Now?"

"Not yet. But here's what I suggest. Turn yourself in. It'll work in your favor."

"I guess." She stood, reached down to pick up her handbag, and placed it on the desk while she pulled her coat from where it was draped over the back of her chair. The bag teetered on the edge of the desk then toppled over, the contents scattering across the floor.

I squatted to gather them up when I saw what had rolled to a stop against my shoe. An EpiPen.

"You have any allergies, Noreen?" I asked. She was still struggling her way into her coat.

"No."

"So this EpiPen isn't yours?"

"What are you talking about?" She grunted, turning in a circle, trying to shove her arm in the sleeve of her coat, "I don't have an EpiPen."

She finally got her coat on and then rounded the desk to see what I was looking at. She gasped in horror. "That's not mine!"

"It was in your bag." I pointed to her bag that was on its side on the floor. Then peered closer. Just peeking out was a zip-lock bag. Reaching forward, I pinched the corner and tugged it until it spilled out onto the floor. Inside the zip-lock bag was a small brown bottle and a syringe. "What's that?" I asked Noreen.

She frowned and leaned down for a closer look. "I've no idea."

I did. I would bet my Keurig, and I don't make that bet lightly, that inside the brown bottle was oyster sauce. And the syringe is what she'd used to administer the sauce to the noodle cup that ultimately killed Anita Finley.

I was reaching for my phone when it rang, startling me. My fingers slipped, and the phone crashed to the floor, as I made a grab for it, my foot shot out and kicked it under the desk. I lunged forward, cracking my head on the edge of the desk, which in turn propelled me backward until I landed on my rear, one leg tucked awkwardly beneath me, the other stretched out straight.

Noreen picked up my phone and handed it to me.

"Hello?" I answered just before it went to message bank.

"Everything okay?" Galloway asked. "You sound odd."

"Just the usual. Slipped when I went to answer the phone. Hang on." I clambered to my feet, ignoring the twinge in my hip. "Thanks for calling back."

"Always." I could hear the smile in his voice, and my heart warmed.

"Um, so, I'm here with Noreen Bellamy. I have evidence that she's been embezzling from other clients aside from Finley Constructions, and she's admitted to it."

"Excellent work."

I preened at the praise. "There's more. Her bag fell off the desk, and an EpiPen rolled out. I suspect it belongs to Anita Finley. And, there's a zip-lock bag with a bottle and syringe inside. I haven't opened it, but I'm willing to bet the bottle contains oyster sauce."

"You have been busy."

"I figured I'd bring her to you, save you sending a patrol car." I moved across the office to study a calendar pinned to the wall, but when I glanced over my shoulder at Noreen, she wasn't there. *What the?* Turning, I looked from one end of the converted shipping container to the other. She'd gone! How could she have gone? There were no other exits aside from the one and only door. That's when I noticed it was slightly ajar. She'd snuck out while I was distracted on the phone.

"Shit!" I cursed, flinging the door open and stepping outside just in time to hear Noreen's car start. She spun the wheels, flinging gravel as she sped out of Finley Constructions, fishtailing out the gate.

"Fitz?"

"Sorry. Rookie mistake. I turned my back on her, and she took off."

"The evidence?"

"Still here." I retreated into the office where Noreen's bag and its contents remained on the floor. The zip-lock bag and EpiPen were exactly where I'd left them. I could only assume her car keys had been in her coat pocket.

"I'm on my way. I'll put out an APB on Bellamy, she won't get far."

I'd just hung up when Logan's truck turned into the yard. He pulled up in front of the office, keeping the engine running while he rolled down his window, sitting next to him in the cab was Anita's ghost. I shot a quick look her way before turning my attention back to Logan.

"Audrey? Is everything okay? What are you doing here?"

"I came to talk with Noreen."

He glanced beyond me to the open door of the office, and then to the empty space where Noreen's car had been parked. He raised his eyebrows as if to say *well, where is she?*

"She took off. Logan, I hate to tell you this, but Noreen has been stealing from you. From what I can tell, just over ten thousand dollars has been embezzled from your account."

He blinked, then turned off the ignition. "Thank God."

"What?" Why would he say that? He was happy she'd been stealing from him. He looked at me with exhaustion pulling at his eyes. "I thought it was Tyler. I knew something was up with the accounts; I just didn't know what. Or who."

"What makes you think it was Tyler?"

"He'd been coming here out of hours. And he and Noreen share a desk. I wondered if he'd somehow gotten the passwords or something."

"Was that the secret you were keeping from Anita?"

He jerked back in shock. "She knew?"

Anita looked at him with so much love and compassion my heart hurt. "I wish he'd told me." She said.

"She knew you were keeping something from her. She just didn't know what."

"I didn't want to worry her. And I certainly didn't want to accuse our son if it wasn't him."

"But you thought it could have been him. Not Noreen?"

"Noreen's been managing the business finances for five years. I trust her. Trusted her. But my son had been acting odd lately." He snorted. "Secretive. Like father like son, I guess."

Anita cocked her head. "That's true. He was staying out late or leaving early in the morning, but I thought he was hanging with his friends. I didn't know he'd been coming to the yard out of hours."

I chewed my lip, wondering how much I should tell him. Them. Anita seemed oblivious to what her son had been up to, which means Ben hadn't told her. I did a quick reconnaissance of the area, searching for him, wondering why he wasn't with Anita.

Seeing the indecision on my face Logan opened the truck door, climbing out to stand in front of me. Anita followed. "Just tell me. Tell me everything. I'd rather know than not."

"I've got no proof..." I hesitated.

"But you have a theory. Is this about who killed Anita?"

"You found my killer?" Anita asked eagerly.

"I'm really not sure." I glanced back at the office

where the zip-lock bag and EpiPen were waiting. It sure looked like Noreen had killed Anita, and her fleeing backed that up, yet she'd seemed genuinely surprised those items were in her bag. And if she had killed Anita, wouldn't you get rid of the evidence and not cart it around with you?

"Audrey?" Logan prompted, snapping me out of my pondering.

"Right, sorry. Yes, about Tyler. I have a suspicion he's in a relationship with Lacey Stevens."

Logan staggered back as if I'd punched him in the face. "Tyler and... Lacey? But she's..."

"Forty-seven. And Tyler's twenty. As I said, I have nothing to back that up at this stage." I warned when I saw Logan's fingers curl into fists. "But it may explain Tyler's behavior. Sneaking around to be with her, trying not to get caught. All adds to the excitement."

"I warned Anita about becoming friends with her." Logan kicked at the ground, frustration giving his voice a hard edge. "She's bad news."

I risked a glance at Anita, who'd frozen in place, her face one of absolute shock.

"Oh?" Intrigued, I leaned closer. Logan looked at me and nodded. "Oh yeah. When she first came to town, I was doing a job at the Hotel and ran into her."

"And?"

"And she propositioned me. Said she could get staff rates on a room at the hotel. Invited me to join her."

My eyes rounded. I hadn't expected that. "Did you tell Anita?"

"Of course."

"And yet she became friends with a woman who'd made it blatantly clear that she fancied her husband."

Logan nodded, face grim. "Like I said, I warned her. But Anita is the forgiving sort. Was the forgiving sort. Lacey was new in town, and Anita felt bad that she didn't know anyone or have any friends. So she took her under her wing."

"Did Lacey try anything again? With you?"

He shook his head. "No, thank goodness. Seems she turned her attention to my son instead."

CHAPTER FOURTEEN

"You need to calm down," I whispered out the corner of my mouth as Anita stormed back and forth in front of me, glowing an angry shade of red. She'd ranted and raved a solid five minutes about what she was going to do to Lacey when she caught up with her. All empty threats, of course, considering she was incorporeal, but I got it. Your best friend messing with your kid was enough to send anyone off the deep end.

Logan had taken the truck over to the lumber storage shed and was loading up while we waited for Galloway. I'd told him he couldn't go in the office until the police arrived, and he'd said he had too much nervous energy to sit and wait, so loading lumber seemed the logical thing to do. I waited out front with Anita.

"Have you seen Ben?" I asked.

"No. Why?"

"He was coming to tell you about Lacey. That we think maybe Tyler took your necklace and gave it to her as a gift."

Anita's face fell. I can't imagine the hurt of having your child steal from you, let alone give that item as a gift to someone else. Someone who was your best friend who was betraying you behind your back.

"Why did you become friends with her, anyway?" I asked. "Especially when you knew she tried to get your husband into bed."

"Oh, I'm not one for grudges. Not usually." She added, clearly thinking about the situation with Tyler. "I trust my husband. He told me straight away what had happened. This sort of thing does crop up now and then in his line of work. He'll turn up to a client's house, and it's some bored housewife looking for a little fun, she tries it on. Logan's a silver fox for sure, I'm aware women find him attractive." She narrowed her eyes. "I wonder if this is why Lacey kept trying to undermine our marriage. She was the one pushing the idea that Logan was having an affair." Then her eyes widened. "She was trying to break us up!"

"But why? If she was in a relationship with Tyler?"

"I don't know. But what you saw at the restaurant this morning, them arguing, you said it sounded like they'd broken up?"

"Seemed that way."

"You don't think she killed me, do you?" Anita whispered, hand over her mouth in horror.

"I can't rule her out. Although it seems extreme. While she had the opportunity, I'm not clear on what her motive would be. She didn't need you out of the way to continue a relationship with Tyler."

"What if it's not Tyler that she wants? What if it's Logan? And she figured the only way she could get him was to get rid of me?"

I couldn't discount it. Not until we'd talked with Lacey. And Tyler. And find out exactly what had been going on. Ben and I could have totally gotten the wrong end of the stick, all of this was entirely speculation, and we could be accusing Lacey of something she hadn't done.

"Even if she did, it was for nothing. Logan would never be with her. He said there was something about her he didn't like, he tolerated her for my sake, but that was it." Anita continued, not waiting for a response.

Galloway's car turned into the lot, and Anita squinted at it for a second before turning back to me. "I bet Ben has gone to find Lacey, see what she's really up to."

"Possibly." I agreed.

"I'm going to find him." With that, she disappeared, leaving me to greet Galloway on my own.

"Fitz." Galloway winked as he climbed out of the car.

"Galloway." I grinned, then pointed to the office door. "Inside, on the floor."

He pulled a couple of evidence bags from his pocket, snapped on a pair of latex gloves, and opened the door. I stood in the doorway and watched as he scooped up the EpiPen and sealed it in an evidence bag, then did the same with the zip-lock bag.

"She did a runner, huh?" He asked, straightening.

"She fooled me," I admitted. "I thought she was going to turn herself in. For the embezzling." I added. "But then her bag fell off the desk and... well, I guess she figured having those in her possession made her look guilty. Of murder."

"I'll get them fingerprinted, see what comes up." He righted Noreen's handbag and collected her belongings that had scattered around it, dropping them back inside. "We'll also do a thorough inspection of her bag and its contents." He explained, "see if she's hiding anything. You said you had further evidence of her embezzling?"

I told him about the historical society accounts and that Noreen had confessed to the thefts when I confronted her.

Gathering up the handbag and two evidence bags, Galloway shook his head. "What was she thinking? She had to know eventually she'd get found out."

"Right? She started skimming to fund a cruise, which, ironically, she hasn't taken. I'm pretty sure the money is all sitting in her account."

"That's something, I suppose. We can make sure it gets back to the clients she stole from."

"What happens next?"

"We'll get the forensic accounting team in the city to go through all of Noreen's accounts and the accounts of all of her clients, big or small. Then once we've confirmed what you've told us, we will lay charges."

"And the EpiPen? The bottle and syringe?"

"The lab can confirm if the bottle contains oyster sauce and if it's the same oyster sauce used in the noodle cup. They can also confirm if the syringe has been used. And like I said, we'll dust for prints."

"Do you think they were planted? That you won't find any prints because they've been wiped clean?" I recalled the look of surprise on Noreen's face. Either she was a damn fine actor, or she'd had no idea those items were in her bag.

"What do you think?"

"I think she's being framed. If Noreen was the one who spiked the noodle cup, she wouldn't have left those things in her bag, she would have disposed of them. She knows how to hide her tracks; she's been doing it with her embezzling. Granted, not very well, but well enough that her clients didn't notice." I chewed on my lip. "What about Keagan? Could he have done this?"

"Anything is possible at this stage. He's been charged with art fraud, but unless one of the clients he sold a forgery to comes forward, those charges may not stick."

"What? That's crazy."

"He's claiming the paintings we found in his home studio are reproductions, not forgeries."

"But what about the two hundred-million-dollar concert painting?"

"We're trying to get the DA to accept a receiving stolen goods charge. It's murky. Anita didn't know the painting was stolen or valuable. She wasn't the owner per se, the historical society is as per the wording of Kelsh's estate. The historical society gave the painting to Keagan for restoration. It's up to us to prove that he knew what it was and was preparing to sell it on the black market. We're also digging into Dudley Kelsh's background. He may well be the initial thief."

I whistled. "And can you? Prove Keagan was up to no good?"

"We're working on it. He had already started on a forgery of the painting, we assume to give to the historical society, covering his tracks. Even if someone recognized the painting in the future, it could be examined and ruled a reproduction, leaving Keagan in the clear because they'll assume the forgery came from the Kelsh estate and wasn't created after the original was found. But we're going through phone and email records, bank accounts, everything. He'd have made contact with a buyer as soon as he got his hands on it. Several, I'd imagine. And sell it to the highest bidder. Once we find a record of those transactions or communications, we've got him."

"Do you think he killed Anita?"

He heaved a sigh. "Well, if she found out the truth about the painting, then he certainly had a motive. He definitely had the opportunity. As did Noreen. We just need evidence. The EpiPen and the syringe and bottle may just give us what we're searching for, a print, even a partial will help. A little bit of DNA, like a drop of sweat. A hair or fiber. Something tying one of them to these items." He held up the evidence bags. "And then we've got them."

"I've got another suspect you might want to take a look at." I glanced over my shoulder. Logan was still loading his truck, out of earshot. "This isn't confirmed, but I have my suspicions."

Galloway headed out the door to place the evidence in his car. "Who?"

I followed, filling him in on the whole story of Lacey and Tyler, ending with, "and now Ben and Anita are both off seeing what they can dig up on the pair."

Slamming the trunk closed, he leaned on it and studied me. "You have been busy."

"I know, right?" I grinned. It was good to see him, I'd missed him last night. My heart was all aflutter, and despite the fact we were investigating a murder, I was giddy with excitement. Or it could be nerves for the PI exam.

As if reading my mind, he said, "I'm glad I got to see you before your exam." His full mouth showed traces of a smile that reached all the way up to his sparkling grey eyes, the blue and steel flecks brilliant in the sunlight.

"Oh? Why's that?" Acting coy was so unlike me I took myself by surprise, almost snorting.

"So I can do this." He offered me a soft kiss, his mouth brushing across mine before he showered tiny kisses along my cheek to my ear. His warm breath stirred my hair as he whispered, "I've missed you."

It was like he was in my head. "I missed you too," I admitted. Corny, but true. He raised his hand to caress my face, and a hunger flashed in his irises, causing an answering warmth to flood my entire body. Wrapping my arms around his neck, I raised myself on tiptoes, my lips a scant inch from his when the blaring of my alarm jerked us apart.

Galloway held up my phone, swiped to turn the alarm off, then handed it to me. I gasped. "You had your hand in my pocket, and I didn't even feel it." I paused. "Do it again."

He laughed and swatted my rear. "You have an exam to get to, remember?"

"That was my one-hour reminder. There's plenty of time."

"One hour?" Galloway cocked his head. "Are you sure?"

"What do you mean?"

"Audrey, it's one-forty-five. You have fifteen minutes."

"What? No way!" I looked at the time on my phone. Holy crap, he was right. Where had the time gone? And what happened to my alarm, I swear I set it for one o'clock.

Grabbing my shoulders, Galloway gave me one more hard kiss, then spun me around and pointed me at my car. "Go. Call me when you're finished."

"Will do." Much like Noreen had, I left the Finley Construction lot with tires spinning and gravel flying.

This couldn't be happening. Slamming my fist on the steering wheel, I peered at the dash. The gas tank was empty. Empty! Where was the screech and flashing light to warn me? Nowhere to be found. Maybe it had absconded with my gas. With no warning that my tank was low, the needle had moved beyond empty, well and truly into the red without so much as a squeak. With no juice, I had no power steering, so with both hands gripping the steering wheel in a death grip, I coaxed my rolling car onto the verge and finally came to a stop.

Grabbing my bag, I slung it over my shoulder, locked the car, and ran as fast as my legs could carry me toward the Council Chambers. I daren't look at the time, I was already cutting it fine. My exam could be overseen by anyone, and I'd initially thought sitting it at the police station was a good idea until Ben pointed out how distracting that would be. And potentially noisy. The next best place had been the Council Chambers, and for a fee, they were happy to accommodate me.

Sweat trickled down my back, and my breath was rasping in and out of my lungs, my bag thumping into my hip with each lunge forward. I skidded around a corner, almost lost my balance, but righted myself and surged onward, the Council Chambers in my sights. Flying up the stairs, I burst through the doors, breathless, red-faced, and disheveled.

"Audrey..." I panted, leaning on the counter, trying to catch my breath, "Fitzgerald."

The woman behind the counter looked at me then turned her attention to the monitor angled to the right of her. "Ah yes. Audrey Fitzgerald, invigilator services. You are aware there is a fee?"

"Yes." I puffed, already reaching into my purse for my wallet, flipping it open and pulling out a fifty. "Here."

While she typed up my receipt and put the money in the cash tin, I looked at the clock on the wall behind her, the second hand sweeping up, in a matter of seconds it would be two o'clock.

A door leading towards the back of the building opened, and a gray-haired man stepped through. "Louise is there an Audrey Fitzgerald he—oh. Are you

Audrey?" He asked, spying me brushing my hair back from my overheated face. I'm sure I was glowing as red as a tomato thanks to the mammoth run I'd taken to get here on time. I nodded.

"Please, come on through. We'll get you set up, and then it's go time. Can I get you anything? Water?"

I could have kissed him. "Water would be wonderful, thank you. Sorry, I rushed to get here."

He smiled reassuringly. "Well, you made it, so you can relax. The exam is delivered online, we can start it at any time, so take a minute to gather yourself, I'll get you a glass of water. Do you need the bathroom?"

I didn't, but as soon as he suggested it, the sudden urge to pee hit me. Nervous wees. I used the bathroom, drank a glass of water, handed over my bag, and was led into a room that held a bank of computers, each with a screen separating them from each other in individual little cubicles. Frank, for I'd learned that was his name, pointed to the cubicle at the far end, next to the window.

"We've got you set up down here. You'll find a pencil and some scrap paper and a calculator. When you're ready to begin, just hit enter on the keyboard. We have you all logged in and ready to go. Once you hit enter, you have ninety minutes to complete the exam. Questions?"

"I'm all good. Thank you."

Frank settled himself in a chair by the door and

pulled out a John Grisham novel. Pulling out my chair, I adjusted the height, stared at the screen in front of me, then with only a slight tremor in my hand, hit enter.

***

Standing on the steps of the Council Chambers one hour and twenty minutes later, I looked at the printout in my hand and allowed myself a little yip of joy. The benefit of sitting the exam online was I got the results immediately. I was now a bona fide private investigator.

Pulling out my phone, I dialed. "Mom? I passed!"

"Oh, darling, that's wonderful, I'm so proud of you. Your father will be thrilled."

"Yeah, I—"

"Darling, I'm sorry, but now's not a good time. I'll call you back this evening, okay? Ta ta."

Frowning at the screen of my phone, I read the words beneath mom's number. *Call disconnected.* My mom had hung up on me. With a shrug, I tried Laura. No answer. Same with Dustin. I didn't even bother trying Dad, he never answered his cell at work. Blowing out a sigh, I pulled up Galloway's number on the off chance he could speak. Nope. Straight through to message bank.

With only a slight twinge of pique, I continued down the steps of the Council Chambers, stumbled on the last one, and staggered out onto the sidewalk, colliding with a woman walking her dog.

"I'm so sorry!" I exclaimed, righting myself. "Are you okay?"

"I'm fine." She hurried away, dragging the poodle at the end of the leash with her.

Ducking into the bakery a few doors down I grabbed an iced caramel macchiato and a bear claw in way of celebration, then called Triple A. Shoving my mouth full of pastry goodness, I meandered back to where I'd left my car on the side of the road, mulling over the apparently faulty fuel gauge and cursing myself that I hadn't noticed it was getting low. Goes to show how reliant we become on machines. I'd gotten so used to the warning alarm when the tank was getting low that I'd gotten into the habit of not even looking at the gauge.

Within half an hour I'd finished my bear claw and my iced caramel macchiato, I'd had a lovely chat with the Triple A mechanic who'd come to my rescue with a jerrycan of gas and a recommendation to get my car checked out by my mechanic for, he agreed, I should have had plenty of notice that the tank was getting low.

Still on a high from passing my exam, despite having no-one to celebrate with, I headed home. Now that I was a qualified private investigator, a world of databases was now available to me that weren't before.

Databases that made conducting background checks a lot easier and a lot faster.

"Hey, Thor." Greeting my cat with a scratch behind his ears, I headed into my home office, Thor winding his way around my ankles as I went.

"What is that I smell?" he asked. "You've had something sweet. With cinnamon. And almond. Did you bring me some? Where is it?" I'd dropped my bag on the floor by the desk, and he was nose-deep, searching for a treat.

"Sorry, buddy, no treats for you."

His head shot up, and he glared at me. "How dare you?" Flouncing out of the room with his tail in the air, I bit back a giggle, for his round belly poked out on both sides—he definitely needed a diet which negated any guilt I felt about not saving him any of my bear claw.

Firing up the computer, I made a pit stop to the bathroom before returning to begin a background check on one Lacey Stevens. It took longer than expected because first, I had to register—as a bonafide private investigator—to use the various databases. Still, once I'd set up the accounts, it was smooth sailing. The hours were ticking by, and the shadows on the wall told me it was getting late in the afternoon when something popped up on Lacey Stevens. Something very interesting.

For one thing, she was fired from her last job in the

city. And she was suspected of arson, but never charged. It hadn't been proven that she was the guilty party, but it seemed she'd been having an affair with the owner of the restaurant where she was working. When he'd ended the relationship, Lacey had turned all bunny boiler on him, stalking and harassing him until it got to the point where he not only fired her, he got a restraining order against her. And then his restaurant burned down.

Crossing to the whiteboard, I updated the information I had on Lacey. She might be crazy psychotic, but was she a killer? I still couldn't figure out a motive for her, and if Ben or Anita didn't return soon, I'd go talk to her myself and get to the bottom of it.

Returning to the computer, I began a check on Noreen. Now that I had the proper authorization, running checks would be one of the first things I do, I promised myself. I was reading through Noreen's results, nothing shocking there, when Ben returned.

"So?" he asked, laying a hand on my shoulder, making me jump. "How did the exam go?"

I twisted in my seat to smile up at him. "I passed!"

"Woop!" he cheered, "I knew you would. Well done, Fitz. We should celebrate."

My face fell. "I wish. But you're a ghost, how can you celebrate with me? And none of my family are taking my calls—although I did tell Mom."

"Hey, I can still celebrate, I just can't drink, which

means all the more for you. Have you looked outside? The sunset is spectacular. Why not grab a beer and watch the sunset with me on the back deck?"

"That's the best offer I've had all day." I stood, stretching out the crick in my back, and padded through to the kitchen, my shoes long since kicked off and lost beneath the desk. Grabbing a beer, I headed out to the deck. Ben hadn't been wrong, the sky was a work of art, streaks of oranges, pinks, and purples, blended vibrantly across the horizon.

Lowering myself into one of the wooden recliners, I swung my legs up and leaned back, the warmth of the setting sun washing over me. "This is perfect," I sighed, taking a swig of beer.

"It sure is." Ben agreed, taking the seat next to me.

"Can you feel it?" I asked.

"Feel what?"

"The warmth of the sun?"

He turned his head to look at me. "No, Fitz. I can't feel anything." And just like that, his words had my mood plummeting. Was I selfish in keeping Ben here, even though he'd assured me it had nothing to do with me, and it was his own personal choice not to move on? I wasn't sure I was buying it. But I also wasn't sure I was ready to let him go.

"I mean, in the physical sense," Ben continued. "But I can feel emotionally. For example, I can see the sunset, and that makes me feel good. I can remember the physical, I can imagine the heat of it, but it's the emotion, the memories that surface of how many sunsets I've sat here, nursing a beer, winding down from a hectic day, that makes up for not feeling the physical."

I know he meant to be reassuring, that he didn't want me to be maudlin. Still, his words brought back the tragedy of his death, that feeling the sun on his skin and the wind in his hair was no longer an option for him. That he'd never get married, have kids, grow old. I didn't realize a tear had escaped and was rolling down my cheek until he tried to wipe it away. The shot of cold on my heated flesh was startling, and I sucked in a breath.

"Sorry."

I smiled. "It's okay." I took another swig of beer. "Tell me about your day. What did you get up to? Did you find out anything?" Talking about the case was a sure-fire distraction.

He jumped to his feet and started pacing. "I did. I went looking for Anita but missed her at home, but Tyler was there, so I figured I'd hang around, see what I could find out."

"And?"

"He's really good at *Call of Duty*."

"You watched him play video games?"

He had the grace to look sheepish. "For a while."

I shook my head and took another swig. "Please tell me you discovered something."

"Actually, I discovered something really cool!"

"Oh?"

"It's hard to describe, but I can... see... phones."

"I can see phones too, so what?"

"No, I mean, I can, like, go into phones and see the data. Even though I can't physically touch things anymore, it's almost like I can travel the data waves."

I blinked in shock. "That could really come in handy," I said more to myself than to him. No wiretaps. Just send Ben in. "How did you discover that?"

"I was sitting next to Tyler on his bed, he kept checking his phone—I assume to see if Lacey had messaged him. She hadn't. And then he tossed the phone aside, and I automatically went to catch it 'cos he'd thrown it where I was sitting. Of course, it sailed right through me, but as it did, I got this flash, like millions of data transfers all at once, messages, photos, a big jumble of it all."

"Then what?"

"I placed my hand over the phone, just enough so it kinda disappeared beneath the surface, but not all the way through. And if I concentrated, I could control what I saw."

"And? What did you see?" I scooted to the edge of my lounger and swung my feet to the deck.

"Messages between him and Lacey. R rated."

"Urgh."

"And photos."

"Ewwww." I cringed.

"But, I've solved the mystery of the missing necklace."

"It's what we thought, isn't it?"

He nodded. "There's a photo on Tyler's phone of Lacey wearing the necklace."

CHAPTER SIXTEEN

I was thinking of how we could get the necklace from Lacey and back where it belonged when the doorbell rang. Heading inside to answer it, I almost tripped over Thor, who bolted toward the front of the house. "Someone's here, someone's here!" He meowed.

"I know, I know." I laughed, padding to the door and flinging it open, remembering belatedly that I should have checked through the peephole first.

"CONGRATULATIONS!" The crowd screaming at me from my porch startled me so bad I jumped back, tripped over Thor, and landed with a jarring thump on my rear. My beer slipped from my fingers and fell to the floor, rolling away, leaving a trail of beer bubbles as it went. I looked up at my family, who stood frozen in the doorway.

"Thought you'd have at least saved your beer, Audrey." Dustin teased, stepping forward and holding out a hand to haul me to my feet.

"I wasn't expecting to open my door and be yelled at." I protested. Dustin picked up the beer and demolished what was left.

"Sorry, Aud." Laura hugged me. "We didn't mean to scare you. We'll clean that up, don't worry. But more importantly, congratulations, little sis, we are so proud of you."

My smile couldn't get any wider, despite the throbbing in my ass. Did butt cheeks bruise? I must remember to check. Behind Laura and Brad was Mom and Dad, then Dustin and Amanda, and way at the back, Galloway. Their respective children raced past me, dutifully treading in the puddle of beer as they went.

"The whole gang's here." I hugged everyone as they filed past. "We're out back, enjoying the sunset."

"We?" Amanda asked.

Shit. Me and Ben. But I couldn't tell them that. "Me and Thor." I pointed to my cat, who was now on his back, paws in the air, enjoying rather rough belly pats from Madeline, Nathaniel, and Isabelle.

Mom ushered us all out onto the deck, taking over cleaning duties from the beer that had now been trampled through the house. Dad thumped his cooler down, flipping the lid open to reveal cider and beer.

"Thanks, Dad. This is perfect." I grabbed a cider, handed Galloway a beer, then headed down the steps to the grass where the kids were running around like mad things.

"You'd think they'd be tired after a full day at daycare." Laura sighed, watching the youngsters.

"I get tired just watching them."

"Same."

Galloway slid an arm around my shoulders and tucked me into his side. I happily leaned against him. It had been wonderful sitting out on the deck with Ben, but with my entire family and Galloway? It was perfect.

"We've ordered pizza," Dustin said, handing Laura a can of soda. "Hope you didn't have any plans."

"Nope." I grinned. And if I had, I would have gladly canceled them to spend time with my crazy family. "So I take it you were all ignoring me on purpose?"

"Sorry." Laura squeezed my hand. "We wanted this to be a surprise."

"You surprised me all right." I rubbed my butt that now felt kinda numb, and everyone laughed.

"Well done, Audrey." Amanda joined us on the lawn, her heels sinking into the grass. "Your mom is right, we're all very proud of you. None of this can have been easy, not only the workload but you know...Ben."

"Thanks, Amanda." I raised my cider in a silent toast.

The sun continued its slide over the horizon. As the colors faded, we sat along the back deck, watching until the last rays disappeared and the night crept in.

Behind us, the sliding door opened, and Mom said, "okay, everyone, inside. Dinner's ready."

Galloway helped me to my feet, and we dutifully filed inside. My mouth dropped open. Balloons and streamers decorated the dining area, at least ten pizzas stood stacked on the table, along with two bottles of champagne.

"Mom." My eyes filled with moisture, and I blinked to clear my vision.

"Darling, you are worth every effort. I'm sorry you felt like we were all ignoring you today. Because we were," she giggled. "But, we were planning this."

"When did you decide all of this?" I waved my hand at the helium balloons dancing on the end of their weighted ribbons.

"Last night. After the two of you left."

"Your mom called me today to clue me in," Galloway whispered in my ear.

"You guys are the best. I'm so glad to have you as my family."

"Gah," Dustin snorted. "Let's eat before you get all mushy."

The kids were set up with a picnic blanket on the floor, Thor in amongst it all trying to steal as much pizza as possible. No wonder he was getting fat. After the adults were seated at the table, I looked at the empty chair to my left, complete with place settings. "Are we expecting someone else?"

"It's for Ben." Mom paused. "All of this was possible because of him. He deserves a seat at the table." Silence descended, and everyone looked at me, waiting for my reaction. Ben, who was standing a few feet away, gave me the thumbs up. I wished I could tell my family the truth, that his ghost was here, but I wasn't sure they were ready to hear it. I especially suspected Amanda would arrange some sort of mental health intervention if I told her the truth.

Instead, I smiled, pulled out the seat, and said, "of course he deserves a seat at the table." And because I'd made space for him, Ben came and sat next to me. "Thanks, Fitz." I raised my cider to him and toasted. "To Ben." The others scrambled to do the same bottles and glasses clinking as they toasted the ghost of Ben Delaney.

After we'd demolished the pizzas, Mom handed me a small wrapped box. "This is for you. To mark the occasion."

"Mom!" I protested. "You didn't have to get me a present."

"I know we didn't have to. We wanted to. Go on, open it."

I blinked, feeling all misty-eyed again, then ripped open the silver wrapping paper with its matching bow.

Inside was a long slim box. Flipping it open, I gasped. Nestled inside was a smartwatch with a white strap and rose gold face. "It's gorgeous," I whispered.

Mom beamed. "We've all seen you drop your phone a million times, so we figured having a smartwatch would maybe stop you needing to reach for your phone so many times."

"Practical and stylish." I winked at her. "It's perfect, Mom. And Dad. Thank you."

"This is from us." Laura tossed a package at me, and it hit my chest before I could catch it. It was wrapped in children's birthday wrapping paper, and she shrugged when I shot her a look. Tearing it open, I barked out a laugh. Inside was a gag gift — a pen that wrote in invisible ink.

"Every gumshoe needs an invisible pen," Laura giggled.

"Indeed. Thank you, another perfect gift." I smiled so much, my face hurt. Amanda handed me a bigger, elegantly wrapped present. "I figure this might come in handy."

"Thanks, Amanda and Dustin." Tearing away the paper revealed a leather compendium with my initials emblazoned on the front. I ran my hand over it before opening it to reveal the diary inside. "It's lovely, thank you." It was. Each of them had gotten me the perfect present, and it wasn't even my birthday.

"Don't forget me," Galloway said into my ear, surprising me by handing me a box.

"You didn't have to get me anything." I protested, and he laughed. "Sure. I have a feeling I'd never hear the end of it if I didn't."

"True." Tearing into the wrapping paper, my eyes rounded in disbelief at the gift he'd bought me. "A stun gun!" I squeaked in delight. Not only that, a pink one.

"A stun gun and torch." He grinned. "Considering how your shooting practice went, I figured keeping it simple—for now—is an excellent strategy."

"She can't zap herself with that, can she?" Amanda asked. I shot her a frown, although her question wasn't too far off of what I was thinking. But at least if I zapped myself, it wouldn't be as devastating as shooting myself.

"Not if she's careful," Galloway replied.

"Can I see it?" Dustin asked, and I handed it over, watching as it made its way around the table, everyone fascinated by the electroshock weapon. I just hoped I'd never have to use it.

"Why a stun gun and not a taser?" I asked Galloway.

He snorted. "Have you seen you fire a gun? A taser works on the same principle. Allows you to defend yourself from a distance. However, the chances of you hitting who you are aiming at are slim to none. While a stun gun can't be used from a distance, if an assailant gets too close to you, one quick zap will subdue him. Or her. Even a warning zap without making contact can be enough to deter someone from attacking provided it's a quick burst — you don't want to deplete the charge."

"This would have come in handy on Saturday with Mills." It was an offhand comment, but Galloway's face darkened, and his eyes flashed. Ben was eagerly following the stun gun around the table as everyone oohed and ahhed over it.

"It would have been perfect. And Mills would have deserved it one hundred percent."

I squeezed his thigh under the table. Galloway had been furious when he'd discovered what Mills had done and had only just managed to stop himself from rearranging the other man's face... with his fist. But a formal investigation was underway, and Mills would finally get what was coming to him, I was sure of it.

Isabelle chose that moment to start wailing, and Laura rushed to pick her up. "We should get going, it's getting late, and this one is tired." She soothed the rambunctious toddler who settled her head on her mom's shoulder, struggling to keep her eyes open.

"Yes," Dustin stood, "time to get our rug rats bathed and into bed."

"Thanks for coming guys." I smiled and began to clear up the plates when Dustin said, "catch!" and threw the stun gun across the table. It's like my own brother doesn't even know me. Since when can someone yell, *catch,* and then throw something at me and expect me to actually catch it? But instinct had me trying, anyway. Dropping the plates back to the table with a clatter I reached out both hands, made contact with the stun gun, only my grip was awkward, and the gun was facing the wrong way. My way. As the fingers of my left hand wrapped around the grip, the prongs connected with my right forearm, and the world spun off its axis.

There was a cacophony of sound, none of it legible. As two zillion volts tore apart every vein in my body, my skin caught on fire. It melted off my bones, and my hair literally sizzled on my head along with a thousand pop, pop, popping sounds. My internal organs rearranged themselves, each one vying for space in the back of my throat. Pretty sure my ovaries along with all my eggs packed a suitcase and declared they were moving out, there would be no little Audrey's in this lifetime thank you very much.

Time slowed down, each second lasted an hour until my soul was burned to a crisp.

"Damn. Shouldn't have charged it."

"Isn't there a safety switch?"

"Oh my God, would you look at her hair... is that normal?"

"Hey, Fitz. How you doing?" It was Ben's voice I

focused on, for he stroked my hair back from my face, and with his ghostly touch came blessed coolness.

"Do it again," I told him, turning my face toward his hand.

"What?"

"Touch me. Your skin is so cold. It feels good." I sighed. My eyes were still closed, either that or I'd gone blind, but I heard the startled whispers. "Who is she talking to?" "Do we need to call an ambulance?"

"She'll be fine in a minute." Galloway's voice, strong and in command. "Let's just give her some space. Maybe you guys should get your kids home? Read them a nice soothing bedtime story, so they don't remember seeing their Aunt flying through the air?"

Oh, my God. The kids had seen. Oh, the poor babies, I'd traumatized them for life.

"Are you kidding?" Brad said. "They thought it was hilarious. Madeline thinks she was dancing."

I groaned. I wasn't sure what was worse, that my nieces and nephew had seen me stun myself, or that they thought I was performing some sort of weird interpretive dance. Yet another Audrey story for future generations to dine out on.

"Why is she talking to herself like that?" Amanda wanted to know. "Has she acquired a brain injury?"

"She's disoriented, that's all. It'll pass." Galloway replied. "But seriously, you should all go home. She'll be fine, honestly. Let this be a lesson to everyone here tonight — stun guns are not toys. No more throwing them at people."

"Sorry." Dustin sounded truly chastised, and I would have kissed Galloway if my limbs weren't wet noodles. I also had a sneaky suspicion I'd peed myself, for while most of my body felt like a thousand red-hot needles were digging into me, my groin had a sense of soothing relief. A damp soothing relief. I groaned in mortification.

"Audrey?" It was Mom's voice now, I cracked open one eyelid with herculean effort and saw Galloway herding Mom away. "I'll take good care of her, I swear. But it's best if y'all leave. I'm sorry."

"Take care of her," Dad said gruffly, then ushered Mom away. I lay on the floor and listened as my family left, heard the front door close, then Galloway was back, kneeling by my side.

"How you feeling?"

"Like the cheese fell off my cracker." I croaked, blinking at him.

He chuckled. "Well, now you have first-hand experience of what it feels like to be stunned."

"Unfortunately."

"Can you stand?" He asked.

"Are my limbs still attached? I can't feel them."

"Oh, you will." He promised.

"What do you mean by that?" His words had an uncanny sense of timing because just as I asked, I felt the first zing of sensation returning. Pins and needles multiplied by ten thousand. "Holy shit," I whimpered, shaking my hands, trying to dispel the awful feeling. But hey, at least I was moving again.

I struggled upright, glanced down at my crotch, thankful to see I had not wet myself after all. With Galloway's help, I made it to my feet, and he guided me onto a chair. "Sit here and get your bearings." He ordered. "I'll clear up. Although... " he paused in gathering up the dirty dishes, "if this was an elaborate ploy on your behalf to get out of cleaning up, well kudos to you, it worked."

I snorted. "Yeah. You got me." I watched in appreciation as Galloway cleared the table, stacked the dishwasher, gathered up the empty bottles and put them in the recycling bin, and by the time he'd done all that, I was ninety-five percent back to normal.

Placing a steaming mug of coffee in front of me, Galloway took the seat opposite. "Better?"

"Much." I blew on the hot brew before taking a sip. "I had a thought."

"Surprising since you just fried your brain."

I rolled my eyes. "Everyone is a comedian. No, but seriously, I've been thinking about Dudley Kelsh."

"What about him?"

"Where did he get that painting from? He had to know it was there. Is that why he left his estate to the historical society? So it would be found after he'd died."

"You think he was the thief?"

"As bizarre as that sounds, it's possible. I mean, I would never have pegged Keagan as a counterfeiter, but you said he had a full-on production line going on in his home studio, all with the intent of ripping off unsuspecting buyers. You think you're buying a Rembrandt, but in reality, you're buying a Keagandt."

"True."

"And Noreen!" I waved my left hand around, almost knocking my coffee over. "Who would think sweet, little, mild-mannered Noreen was ripping off her clients, stealing from them?"

"Again, true."

"And Lacey Stevens." I stopped short and blew out a breath. "I'm really not sure what to make of her," I admitted. I told Galloway of the background check I'd run on Lacey, how she was fired from her last job and suspected of arson, but no charges had been laid. But her former boss and lover had an AVO against her. "But despite all that, I'm not coming up with a motive for her killing Anita."

"You said she propositioned Logan? Maybe it was that. Maybe it's him she wants, but Logan's a stand-up guy, no way he'd cheat on his wife. Only way to fix that problem?"

"Get rid of the wife."

"Exactly."

"But why is she sleeping with the son?" That's what had me puzzled. Did she start up an affair with Tyler in the hopes of making his dad jealous? But it kinda defeated the point if Logan didn't even know about it. Stifling a yawn, I scratched at my head, then, realizing something wasn't quite right with my hair, I patted all over my head, my eyes widening in horror. "What's happened to my hair?" Shooting up from the table, I raced to the bathroom.

"Holy shit." My reflection confirmed it. I was now sporting an eighties frizzy, crimped style. Galloway came up behind me, smiling over my head at my reflection in the mirror. "I like it. It looks kinda sexy."

"Pft, you're deluded." But I turned my head from side to side, trying to see the allure, not sure if he was serious or pulling my leg. Then I got distracted by his hands as they slid down my arms and across my abdomen.

"I could use a shower." I breathed.

With his mouth on my neck, his voice vibrated through me. "I like where this is going."

"Me too." Turning in his arms, I wrapped my arms around his neck, and he effortlessly lifted me. My legs clamped around his waist, my mouth fused to his, and this time when the world spun, it was in a good way.

CHAPTER SEVENTEEN

"*B*ack again so soon?" The waitress at the Firefly Bay Hotel Restaurant smiled, tablet at the ready to take my order.

"Yesterday's breakfast was to die for." I smiled in return, "I couldn't resist coming back." Plus, I still hadn't done my grocery shopping. But I had another reason for choosing this particular establishment to quench my need for food. I was determined to get to the bottom of the enigma of Lacey Stevens.

"What can I get you today?"

"I'll have the pancakes."

"With bacon?"

"Yes, please. And coffee. Black."

"Coming right up." Before she could turn away, I added, "before you go, is Lacey Stevens working today?"

"Yes, she's the chef this morning. She's on breakfast and lunch all week."

"I was wondering if it was possible to have a word with her?"

The waitress frowned. "Well... she is working, but I can let her know you'd like to speak with her. Is there a problem?"

"Oh no, no, nothing like that."

The waitress nodded. "Okay. I'll let her know. Your order won't be long."

My coffee arrived, and while I savored the lifesaving capabilities of caffeine, I eyeballed Ben, who was flitting from table to table, checking out what everyone was having for breakfast. He'd been obsessed with food lately, and I wondered if he'd been watching a bit too much of Master Chef.

The kitchen door swung open, and I glanced over, surprised to see Lacey step through, carrying what I assumed to be my order. Hot on her heels? Anita.

Sliding my pancakes in front of me, Lacey straightened and wiped her hands on the white apron she wore. "I heard you wanted a word. I can spare you a minute."

"I'll make it quick," I promised. "Did you kill Anita Finley?"

She snorted, not surprised in the least by my question. Pulling out the chair opposite, she sat. "No, I did not."

"But, you are having an affair with her son."

"There's no law against two consenting adults having sex." She shot back.

"No, there isn't. But Anita was your friend. Why would you have a relationship with her son? And I hear you propositioned her husband, too."

Heaving a sigh and rolling her eyes to the ceiling, Lacey placed her palms on the tabletop and leaned toward me. "I'm a woman of a certain age who has needs. It is absolutely no one's business how I have those needs met. Sleeping with Tyler has nothing to do with Anita."

"But why? Why Tyler?" I needed to understand.

"He's gorgeous, and he's young." Her voice dropped. "Young men have stamina."

Anita gasped in what I guessed to be outrage, but I ignored her. Lacey continued. "When I first laid eyes on Logan, yes, of course, I tried it on. The man is gorgeous—I can see where Tyler got his looks from. And hey, if he'd agreed to a dalliance, I was totally okay with that, but it wouldn't have meant anything. Sex is just sex."

"It is not!" Anita protested. "It's an act of love between two people."

"And that?" I pointed to the diamond pendant I could see nestled beneath her button-down blouse. The one Anita had hired me to find.

"Is this what this is all about? This damn

necklace?" Lacey did the one brow arch thing, and I did my best not to let it distract me—how did people do that?

"Here. Take it." Lacey tugged the chain from around her neck, tossing the necklace on the table. "Tyler gave it to me as a gift. At the time, I didn't know it was Anita's precious necklace."

"Would it have mattered if you'd known?" I gathered the necklace into my palm and closed my fingers over it.

Lacey shrugged. "Believe it or not, my friendship with Anita had nothing to do with Tyler and vice versa. She was my friend, and I will miss her." To my utter surprise, Lacey's eyes misted, and she fanned her face before the tears filling her eyes could spill over.

"Well." Anita huffed, taken aback. I glanced at her, but Anita was studying her friend intently. "I don't think it was her," she finally said, crossing her arms over her chest. I wasn't so sure.

"I know you've probably checked me out," Lacey sniffed, wiping under her eyes, "so you know what happened at my last job..."

"Your affair with your boss and burning his restaurant down?" I quizzed.

She stiffened. "Oh, the affair happened all right, but none of that went down the way he said it did. He chased me. He instigated everything, and it was fun while it lasted, but I dumped him. He was the one who couldn't let go. He was the one who got all bent out of shape and made up outrageous allegations that I was stalking and harassing him. I wouldn't be surprised if he burned his own restaurant down."

"Why move away then, if you were innocent?"

"Hello! Mud sticks. He wanted to hurt me, but when nothing he did worked, he lied to the police and got an AVO taken out against me. No way anyone was going to hire me once word got out about that, despite it being totally bogus."

"Oh, Lacey," Anita sighed, "that's awful, honey. Why didn't you ever tell me that?"

"Did Anita know any of this?" I dutifully asked.

Lacey hunched a shoulder. "The past is in the past. I'm in Firefly Bay for a fresh start, no need to bring all that baggage with me."

"Why didn't you give the necklace back to Tyler? When he asked?"

"To punish him for stealing it from his mom in the first place. I had every intention of returning it, I too would like to see her buried wearing it, I'm not heartless."

"Oh," Anita whispered.

"So you and Tyler..."

Lacey glanced out the window. "We're finished. It was fun while it lasted, but his mom dying? I'm no good with all of that emotion, you know? I can't help him with his grief. He needs a girlfriend for that, and that wasn't what I was. Plus... I need to grieve for my friend too, and ending things with Tyler seemed like the right thing to do... in the end."

I wanted to say that perhaps the right thing to do would have been not having an affair with your best friends' son to begin with, but I bit my tongue. You can't take back the past, no matter how hard you try.

Lacey stood. "I've gotta get back to work. Was there anything else?"

"No. Thanks for talking with me." Anita and I watched as she walked away, then I pulled out my phone and put it to my ear.

"Well?" I asked Anita. "What do you think?"

"I was so angry with her. So angry." Anita slid into the chair Lacey had vacated. "And I haven't forgiven her for sleeping with my boy. But I understand. Lacey made no secret of the fact that she had a very strong appetite when it came to men. I know she'd had one-night stands with guests from the hotel before. And she hadn't known about the necklace."

"So she says."

"I believe her." Anita glanced at my pancakes. "You better eat those before they get cold. She really is an exceptional cook."

After leaving the Hotel, I strolled along the boardwalk with the idea I'd walk off the hundred pounds I'd just put on when I bumped into Bob Moore and Ron Holt, members of the historical society, carrying fishing poles.

"Gentlemen," I greeted. "Nice day for it."

"Morning," Bob stopped and put his tackle box down, Ron followed suit. "You're Audrey, right? The gal who's helping with the Kelsh estate."

"Correct. Although the place is a crime scene now."

"Did you see the news?" Ron asked, "that Keagan knew the painting Anita found out there was worth millions? And that he lied to us about it."

I nodded. "I heard."

"The society has really taken some hits over the last few days." Bob shook his head as if unable to believe the goings-on of late.

"I think Mary has everything under control," I smiled. "She said something about elections."

Bob and Ron glanced at each other.

"What? What does that look mean?" I demanded.

Bob shook his head again. "Mary has been desperate to be president of the society for years. She's self-nominated how many times now, Ron? Three? Four?"

"Four, I think." Ron joined in the nodding.

"And what? No one voted for her?" I asked.

This time they shook their heads.

"Why not?"

"Well, Anita was such a good president. Why would we vote for someone else?"

"Oh, so there wasn't an actual vacancy?"

"Every two years, we have to open up the committee to new members. This includes all the official positions like president, treasurer, secretary," Ron said.

"And every time, the same people get voted in." Bob supplied.

"So Mary has never moved from her position as secretary of the society?"

"Nope." Ron was back to nodding. Then he turned to Bob. "Guess she might be in luck this time around? With both the president and vice-president positions vacant."

Anita groaned. "They're right, you know. Mary will be pleased."

"I saw her at the society yesterday." It was my turn to nod. "She said she was getting ready for the elections."

"She means well." Anita sighed. "She's just a tad overbearing. The trouble is, over the years, she's managed to get pretty much every single committee member offside, so of course, none of them will vote for her."

"Will that change now, do you think?"

"It all depends on whether someone else is

nominated." Anita shrugged. "If no one else wants the job, then it'll most likely fall to Mary—we all know she wants it."

"Will what change, love?" Bob asked, which is when I realized I'd been talking with Anita in front of them. *Busted!*

"Sorry," I grinned sheepishly. "I was talking to myself. Sorry, I do that a lot. I must look a bit of a nut."

"Ha!" Ron snorted. "We do that all the time, don't we, Bob?"

"Indeed, we do." Bob chortled. I smiled at the two elderly men, then glanced at my smartwatch. "It's been lovely chatting, but I've gotta run. Good luck with the fishing." I started to back away.

"Will you be joining the committee?" Bob asked before I could leave.

"I'm not sure I'll have the time." I didn't want to hurt their feelings by flat out saying no. Anita glanced at me. "That would be a wonderful idea, Audrey. You should join."

I tried to convey with my eyes that it was absolutely not going to happen. I waved to the men and hurried away before they could hound me into agreeing. Alas, I could not ditch Anita.

"If you were to join the committee," she continued nagging in my ear, "I could help you!"

"Not going to happen," I said from between clenched teeth. Plus, I liked to think that once we solved her murder and her killer brought to justice, Anita would move on. I'm not sure I could cope with the thought of two ghosts haunting me for a lifetime. Not that Ben was an issue. For my own selfish reasons, I liked having him around, but one incorporeal being was enough.

"But, that does give me an idea," I said, returning to my car.

"What's that?" Ben had caught up with us, and the two ghosts made themselves comfortable in my vehicle.

"There's something about Mary." Reversing the car out of its spot, I headed toward home.

Ben guffawed with laughter. "What?" Anita asked, "what's so funny?"

"There's something about Mary?" He gasped through peals of laughter, and I couldn't help but join in.

"It's a movie," I told Anita. "Ben, you're going to have to explain it to her, I absolutely refuse to do it."

While Ben relayed the movie storyline to Anita, I called Galloway.

"Morning, gorgeous." He answered on the first ring.

"Hey, handsome," I grinned. "I missed you this morning."

"Sorry, early start. And you looked so peaceful I didn't have the heart to wake you."

"Naawwww, isn't that cute?" Ben made gagging noises in the background.

"Shut up," I grumbled.

"I hope you're talking to Ben," Galloway replied.

Shit. "Sorry. Yes. He's being juvenile." Ben stuck his tongue out, and I rolled my eyes. Case in point.

"What can I do for you?"

"When you took Noreen's handbag yesterday, did anyone go through it? Was it all logged as evidence?"

"Yes, the bag and its contents were logged. Why?"

"I have a theory." It was an out-there theory, but it was niggling in the back of my brain. My PI training had taught me not to ignore those niggly little feelings, nor the annoying voices, although right now those annoying voices belonged to two ghosts. "Would you two please shush?" I hissed at them.

"Sorry." Anita immediately complied.

"Can I help it if she wants a blow by blow account of Something About Mary?"

She gasped. "I do not!"

"Do too!"

"Guys! Please! Why don't the two of you go on ahead, huh, and let me talk to Galloway in peace?"

"Splendid idea, Fitzgerald." Ben winked, and the two of them disappeared. I turned my attention back to the phone. "Sorry. Two ghosts discussing movie plots do not make it easy to have a conversation."

Galloway laughed. "I take it they've gone?"

"They have."

"Right, so tell me about this theory of yours."

"Was there a single earring in Noreen's bag? Specifically, a pearl one?"

"Hang on, lemme check." I could hear him typing, then a few seconds of silence as he read whatever appeared on his screen. "Actually, there was. Why?"

"Do you know what strikes me as odd about that?"

"What, that a woman has a stray earring in her handbag? Maybe she took it off to talk on the phone, or maybe she just lost one and took the other out, so she's not walking around with one earring?"

"Both valid reasons." I agreed. "But Noreen Bellamy does not have pierced ears."

Silence for a moment, then Galloway said, "it's not her earring."

"Correct."

"But you know who's earring it is, I'm assuming?"

"I think so. What about the EpiPen and syringe? Did you get prints?"

"Nah, they'd been wiped."

I shook my head with a sigh. "I really don't think Noreen is the killer. Why would you go to the trouble of wiping your prints off the murder weapon and then leave it in your handbag?"

"Agreed. I'd say it was planted."

"What does Noreen say about it?"

"She's confessed to embezzling but categorically

denies spiking Anita's food and stealing her EpiPen. I'm inclined to believe her. There's nothing to suggest that Anita was on to her. Noreen kept delivering altered profit-and-loss statements to the committee, and they were buying it. Noreen had no motive to want Anita dead. Plus, the committee wasn't Noreen's only victim. Any of her clients could have suspected she was stealing from them, what was she going to do, kill them all?"

Fair point. "And Keagan?"

"Same story. Anita, in particular, had no reason to distrust what Keagan had told them about the painting. Neither she nor the committee had been sniffing around asking questions. Plus, he'd almost finished with the reproduction he was going to give them. If we hadn't have caught him, it would have all gone to plan, so again, no motive for him to have killed Anita."

There was a moment's silence, then Galloway asked, "how did it go with Lacey? You went to see her?"

"I did. I got Anita's necklace back." I patted my pocket where I'd tucked the pendant. Logan and Tyler would be pleased to have it returned. I filled Galloway in on everything Lacey had told me.

"So our three prime suspects are looking innocent," Galloway said.

"I've got a new lead. It could be nothing, though," I added hastily.

"Is this about the earring?"

"Yeah. I think it belongs to Mary Wilson." Flashbacks of when I'd first gone to the historical society this morning popped into my head, and I was sure Mary had been wearing both earrings, yet when I'd returned later, only one.

"And she is?"

"The secretary of the historical society. A woman who is, it seems, desperate to be the president."

"And you think she killed off the current president so she could take her place?" His voice belied just how far-fetched he thought that theory was.

"Stranger things have happened." I shot back. "But finding her earring in Noreen's bag means nothing. Noreen may have found it on the ground and picked it up, recognizing it, and intending to return it to Mary. Or Mary could have been standing next to Noreen when it fell off, and it landed in her bag. It could mean absolutely nothing."

"I'll ask Noreen about it, see if she knows how it came to be in her bag," he said.

After hanging up, I pondered what I knew about Mary Wilson, and it wasn't much. She was in her mid-sixties, a round woman with arthritic knees who got around on a canary yellow mobility scooter. I remember Anita introducing me to Mary at Friday night's dinner, and yesterday she'd given me free rein to the society's computer, not the actions of someone with something to hide.

Back at home, I hurried into my office and pulled up the files I'd copied on to the USB.

"What's up?" Ben asked, hovering behind me and reading over my shoulder.

"I'm searching for anything that Mary was involved in. With the society." I added.

"Mary was involved with all of our projects," Anita said, hovering over my other shoulder. Between the two of them, an icy chill was snaking up my spine.

"How involved?"

"What do you mean?" I could hear the puzzlement in Anita's voice and glanced at her. "Was Mary running any of the projects or events? What was she responsible for?" For it struck me if Mary was gunning for presidency, she'd have her finger in every pie available.

"Oh, right. Ummm, let me think. You see..." I could feel the air shift behind me, knew Anita was pacing. "Mary is a very enthusiastic member of the society."

"So I understand."

"But as president, I took the lead on most—if not all—events."

"Was there any in particular that Mary was more passionate about? That maybe she pushed you to let her run?"

"Why? What are you getting at?" Ben asked.

"Bob and Ron said that Mary was keen to step up. That she had her sights set on being president of the historical society."

"Yes, yes, that's true," Anita confirmed what I already knew. Then she froze and looked at me aghast. "You don't think this was Mary? That she killed me so she could become president?"

I shrugged. "I want to know if there was anything she was working on or wanted to work on, but was denied, that pushed her over the edge. That made her take action. Against you."

Ben nodded, crossing his arms over his chest. "You're looking for a motive. Outside of the general 'she wants to be president' thing."

"Yes. Why now? If it was her, why now? What changed?"

"And you think a clue is in the historical societies files?" He quizzed.

I turned back to the screen. "I hope so."

"Oh," Anita whispered. I swiveled to look at her. "You thought of something?"

She nodded, hand over her mouth, eyes wide.

"What is it?" I asked.

Dropping her hand, she said softly, "it was the carousel. The restoration of the carousel. Mary's grandfather built it. She wanted to lead the restoration of it."

"But?"

"But I told her it wasn't necessary because Logan was a carpenter, and between him and Tyler, they could take care of it, we didn't need her input."

"Ouch," Ben hissed.

Anita looked distraught. "How could I have been so insensitive? I remember it now. The meeting where we discussed it. Mary brought all these original photographs, taken when the carousel was first built. She was so proud. And I dismissed her. It wasn't a priority, we had so much going on that I waved her aside and said Finley Constructions would take care of it. I didn't even look at the photographs."

"When was that?"

"Last month." She pointed to the list of files on the screen. "It should be documented in last month's minutes."

I opened the document and scanned through the transcript of the minutes. A scant sentence had been written about the carousel restoration. "And Mary takes the minutes?"

"She does."

"And have these been distributed? Or do you read through them at the next meeting?"

"No, they get distributed as soon as they're ready, and we pass them at the next meeting. These were sent out last week."

I chewed my lip. "But it wouldn't have come as a shock to Mary. She was the one who took the minutes.

But I think we can agree that the carousel was probably a stressor for her."

"I feel awful," Anita whispered, and Ben slung a comforting arm around her shoulders. "She worked hard for the society, and I disregarded her input on something very dear to her."

"I'm going to talk to her." Snatching up my bag and keys, I headed back out. I was reasonably confident mild-mannered Mary Wilson was our killer.

CHAPTER EIGHTEEN

"Back again, dear?" Mary was exactly where I expected her to be. At the historical society. I found her in the boardroom, photographs of the carousel spread out over the large oak table.

"I see you're working on the carousel." I nodded toward the photographs.

"Yes, yes," she rose to her feet and smiled. "It's a project dear to my heart."

"I hear your grandfather helped build the original?"

"Helped?" She stiffened. "He built it himself."

"Sorry, my mistake." I wandered to the opposite side of the table and looked at the black and white prints. "He was clearly a very talented craftsman." I picked up a yellowed sheet of paper, on it, the hand-drawn design for the carousel.

Mary's eyes locked on to the blueprint in my hand. "Yes. He was."

"Must have annoyed you to have the project handed over to Finley Construction with no input from you."

She sniffed. "Somewhat. Do you mind putting that down? The paper is very old, it's quite delicate."

"Right." I placed the document back on the table. "Is that why you killed Anita?"

She didn't so much as blink. "I didn't intend to kill her. I just wanted her out of commission for a while."

"Why?"

"So that her husband would stay home and take care of her."

The penny dropped. "Leaving the restoration project to you. Why didn't you want Finley Constructions to work on it?"

"It wasn't that I didn't want them, per se. I just wanted a say in who we hired. I wanted someone who would be interested in looking at these—" she waved at the photographs on the table. "Someone who appreciated the historical relevance, that would care. To Anita's husband, it was just another job."

"He didn't want to see the original blueprints?" That surprised me. For someone undertaking a restoration project having the original design to work from would be priceless.

Mary couldn't meet my eyes, and as I continued to study her, I realized the truth. "You didn't give him a chance, did you? Did you even tell Anita these existed?"

"I tried to!" She exclaimed. "At the last meeting, but she was in too much of a hurry, more interested in talking about the Kelsh estate than anything else. When it was time to discuss the carousel, she just said that Finley Constructions will take care of it at a discounted rate. Before I could blink, she'd moved on to the next item on the agenda."

"This is all my fault," Anita whispered. She and Ben had joined me, and while I'd been talking with Mary, Anita had been studying the old photographs. "These really are magnificent, and I paid her no heed. She's right. I didn't give her a chance. And Logan would have loved to have seen the original blueprints. He still can. You'll tell her that, right?"

"So, what happened? You slipped back here after Friday night's dinner and dosed one of the noodle cups. How did you know Anita would take them?"

"I overheard her and Lacey talking. Anita said she may drop in and pick them up the next day when she headed out to the Kelsh estate, but only if no one else wanted them."

Anita gasped. "That's right. I did. I'd forgotten that."

"When did you steal her EpiPen?"

"Friday night at the dinner. I was watching her and Lacey talking with you. You'd just taken a mouthful of Eleanor's seafood surprise. That's when the idea hit me. I could use Anita's allergy against her. Make her sick. I knew Lacey always made a lot of noodle cups because Anita liked them so much, so that part was easy. I knew she carried her EpiPen with her everywhere, so it was simple enough to duck into the cloakroom and take it from her purse."

"And put it in Noreen's."

She snorted. "Actually, no. I didn't put that stuff in Noreen's bag until yesterday. All this time, I thought Anita had been exaggerating when she said her allergy was deadly. I put just the tiniest drop of oyster sauce on that noodle cup. Turns out, she was right. Without her EpiPen..." she sighed. "Well, I couldn't take it back, could I? What's done is done. So I had to get rid of the evidence. I figured the police would be by sooner or later, so when Noreen came in, I waited until she went to the kitchen to make a coffee. I slipped the EpiPen and oyster sauce into her bag."

"You know something, Fitz?" Ben, who'd been standing behind Mary, said to me over her shoulder. "She's giving this up way too easily. And look how calm she is. She's not distraught. No tears. No remorse."

He had a point. I kept my eyes on Mary but listened to Ben and Anita, who asked, "what does that mean?"

"It means she doesn't intend for Audrey to repeat this. Fitz, you need to get out of here."

I stiffened. He was right. I'd been lulled into Mary's sweet little old lady persona. Still, intentionally or not, she'd killed a woman, yet here she stood, calm as a cucumber, telling me all about it. And just as soon as I'd thought it, Mary surprised me by pulling a gun.

"Whoa!" I held up both hands, surprised beyond measure that this round, harmless-looking woman was carrying a firearm. And just where had she been keeping it?

"It's been nice chatting, Audrey, but now it's time to go." She motioned with the gun, indicating I should move my ass toward the door. Digging my heels in, I stayed put.

"It's not too late to fix this," I said.

She laughed. "What? Turn myself in? I don't think so."

"The police already know about you." I blurted. "Notice anything missing?"

"Missing? What do you mean?"

I touched both of my earlobes between my thumbs and index fingers. Holding the gun in one hand, she mimicked the move with the other, freezing when she discovered the missing earring.

"You didn't notice, but when you stashed that stuff

in Noreen's bag, you dropped an earring."

"Pft. Circumstantial."

"Noreen's in custody. Oh, not for Anita's murder, despite your plan to frame her. She's been skimming from her clients' accounts. The historical societies included. And when the police took her in, they discovered the EpiPen, the oyster sauce, and the syringe. But the odd part? They'd been wiped down. No fingerprints. That made them look closer. And that's when they found a pearl earring in her bag."

She clenched her jaw. "Can't prove it's mine."

"It's not Noreen's. She doesn't have pierced ears. And I happened to notice yesterday that you had a missing earring. A missing pearl earring. I'd be willing to bet that earring has your DNA all over it."

That rattled her. She turned her back and began pacing. With her distracted, I took the opportunity to pull the stun gun from my bag and tuck it in the back of my waistband. I'd need to get close enough to use it before she could pull the trigger on the gun. Either that or pray that she was a rotten aim.

"What was that?" She pivoted and raised the gun. "What did you just do?"

"What? Nothing!" I protested.

"Give me your bag." She demanded. "Slide it across the table."

I did as instructed, watched while she dug inside and pulled out my phone, squinting at the screen, seemingly satisfied that it was blank, that I hadn't made a call. Then she threw it on the floor and slammed her heel down on it, the screen crunching under her weight.

"Hey!" I protested. "That was expensive." And the second phone I'd been through in a matter of months.

"Doesn't matter, you won't be needing it where you're going." She jerked the gun at me again. "Get moving."

"You won't get away with this, Mary. Turn yourself in now, before you make matters worse."

"Move!" For the first time in this entire situation, her voice rose, startling me, but I stood my ground. If she intended to shoot me, she was going to have to do it here, not some convenient spot where she could hide the evidence.

"I'm going to see what I can do with this," Ben said, crouching behind Mary.

"With what?" I asked, unable to see what he was up to.

"Your phone. She's busted the screen for sure, but some components inside may still work."

"Who are you talking to?" Mary demanded, looking behind her and then back at me.

"No one."

Anita approached Ben, standing on Mary's other side. "But how will you call for help if you can't touch anything?"

"I discovered I can kinda manipulate technology, like the data itself. I don't understand the science of it, but when I put my hand just inside a phone, I can see everything stored on the phone."

"Really?" Anita sounded excited. "I want to try."

"Guys," I warned. "Now is hardly the time."

"Try on Mary's phone. She's gotta have one here somewhere. I'm going to see if I can send a signal to Galloway."

"Who are you talking to?" Mary demanded again, edging around the table toward me. *Yes, come closer, close enough so I can stun you.*

"You're imagining things," I replied. "I didn't say anything."

She waved the gun, and I almost lunged for it, but she wasn't close enough. Ignoring the trickle of sweat that ran down my back and the thundering of my pulse in my ears, I tried to remain calm and not freak out.

"You're trying to trick me." She accused. One more step. Okay, maybe two, she had short legs.

"How's it going?" I asked Ben, casting a quick glance in his direction before turning my attention back to the approaching grandma brandishing a weapon at me.

"Something's happening, but I'm not sure what." Ben glanced up over the back of the chairs. "It's all static to me, but maybe something will get through.

You okay with her?" He was watching Mary with a frown on his face.

"All good."

"You're doing that to try to distract me!" Mary accused. "Well, it's not going to work, I said move!" Now she was close enough. Reaching my right hand behind my back, I grabbed the stun gun while simultaneously reaching forward with my left to seize her wrist and jerk her arm up, so the gun was aiming at the ceiling and not at me.

We struggled, staggering left, then right. Then I managed to wedge the stun gun between us and press the prongs against her abdomen before squeezing the trigger. She vibrated as eight hundred thousand volts passed through her, and I could almost sympathize. Almost. There was a loud bang as we both toppled backward, her dead weight causing me to lose my footing. We landed with a crash that rattled my teeth.

"Fitz! Are you okay?" Ben was there, trying to haul Mary off me, but his hand just passed right through her.

"Urgh." I grunted, "I'm fine." Wedging my hands against Mary's shoulders, I rolled her off me and struggled to my feet. My stun gun was on the floor several feet away, as was her gun, and I rushed to pick them both up, frowning when a drop of blood dripped onto the carpet.

"What?" I reached down and touched the drop,

then looked back up at the ceiling. I have no idea what I was expecting to find up there, a body strung up to explain the dripping blood, perhaps? Or maybe I'd seen one too many scary movies. Regardless, there was no body on the ceiling, and Mary was making garbled noises on the floor three feet away. So whose blood was this?

"Audrey, you're shot!" Anita gasped.

"What? No, I'm not." I protested. I'd know if I was shot, and I hadn't felt a thing. Although my ears were still ringing from the gun going off, I figure that bullet had gone wide, maybe into the wall or ceiling.

"You're bleeding, Fitz," Ben confirmed, pointing at my arm. I glanced down and almost passed out. There it was, a bullet-shaped furrow across my upper arm, blood not exactly gushing, but a reasonably decent flow. Clamping my hand over the wound, I looked at Ben in horror. "Now what do I do?" I squeaked. Mary wouldn't be out for long, but I knew from experience that it took me a good twenty minutes to shake off the effects of being stunned.

"Secure the weapons, grab a clean tea towel from the kitchen and wrap it around your arm, keeping pressure on the wound to stop the bleeding."

"Right." I tucked my stun gun back into the waistband of my jeans and took the gun with me while I ducked out of the meeting room and into the kitchen, rummaging through the cupboards until I found a neatly folded stack of tea towels.

"Hold this," I said to Ben, passing him the gun, only, of course, he couldn't hold it, and it clattered to the floor. "Shit!" I yelled, hopping aside in case I accidentally shot myself in the leg. Ignoring the gun for now, I snatched up a tea towel and wrapped it around my upper arm, hissing as I pulled it tight.

Rushing back to the boardroom, I checked on Mary, who was still moaning and groaning on the floor, then searched her bag that was hanging off the back of a chair. Bingo, one cell phone.

"Firefly Bay Police."

"Detective Galloway, please."

"One moment."

Ten seconds later, Galloway picked up. "Galloway."

"It's me." I'd never been so relieved to hear his voice. The adrenaline that had been pumping through my system had waned, my arm was throbbing, and the phone in my hand was as heavy as a brick. Pulling out a chair, I sat, resting my elbow on the table.

"Audrey? Why are you calling on the landline?"

"Phone broke."

"What's happened? Where are you?"

I filled him in on what had happened, my voice only a little bit wobbly. After telling me to stay put—as if I had plans otherwise—he hung up, and I sat with Anita and

Ben, watching Mary on the floor. She'd stopped drooling, which was something, and the groaning had stopped too. In the distance, I could hear sirens approaching.

"Hear that, Mary?" I asked conversationally, giving her foot a nudge. "That's the cops coming to arrest your ass."

Her eyes blinked open, and I waited while she fought to focus.

"That's right. You're busted for the murder of Anita Finley. And the attempted murder of moi. I can't believe you shot me, Mary. That was so uncalled for."

Ben snorted, then we both jerked when a bright light filled the room. It was time. Anita's murder had been solved. Time for her to move on.

"Is that for me?" Anita gasped.

Ben nodded. "It is."

"What about you? Are you coming?"

"Nah. I'm good. I'm not done here."

"Bye, Anita." I smiled and gave a little wave.

"Thank you so much. For everything. Keep an eye on my boys, won't you?"

"I will."

Then she stepped forward. "Momma? Is that you?" The light intensified until it was blinding, and I had to look away, my eyes screwed shut.

"She's gone," Ben said. I blinked. Sure enough, the light was gone, and so was Anita, just in time for

Galloway to come bursting in, Young and Walsh hot on his heels, weapons drawn.

After ascertaining Mary wasn't a threat, Walsh holstered his weapon and stuck his head out the door, calling out to the paramedics waiting outside that it was all clear.

"Audrey Fitzgerald, we meet again." One of the paramedics placed his bag on the table and unwrapped the tea towel from my arm to check my wound.

"Jayce." I smiled at him. "This doesn't need a hospital trip, does it? It's just a scratch."

The other paramedic who was checking on Mary glanced up when he heard my name. "Is that you, Audrey? What have you gotten into now?"

"Hey, Ned." I returned his greeting. "Oh, you know, the usual."

Jayce glanced at Ned. "GSW to the upper arm. What you got?"

"No external signs of injury," Ned replied. He nodded toward my injury. "Through and through?"

"Nah, winged her. A few stitches and she'll be as good as new," Jayce said. "What did you do to her, Audrey?"

"Stun gun."

"Ahh." Ned nodded. "I'll check her vitals, but she should be fine."

"Good, because she's under arrest," Galloway

growled. I reached up with my free hand and threaded my fingers with his, squeezing. "It's okay. If it's any consolation, I don't think she meant to shoot me. The gun went off after I tased her."

"She shouldn't have been pointing a gun at you in the first place." He pointed out.

"True." It was also true that Mary hadn't intended to kill Anita, but when that hadn't gone to plan, she hadn't exactly been filled with remorse. In fact, she'd planted evidence to implicate Noreen, and then intended to... what? Kill me to stop me from telling anyone what I'd discovered? It all seemed so extreme over a carousel.

"You better start choosing what steak knives you want," Galloway said, watching while Jayce wrapped a bandage around my arm.

"Huh?"

"Your hospital frequent flyer card is about to get punched. Last time you told me you were one visit away from a free colonoscopy and a set of steak knives." He reminded me, his lips curling up into a cheeky grin.

Jayce barked out a laugh. "That's right, pretty sure that's what you said."

"Not you too," I grumbled with a wink. "I could use the steak knives, though."

"Jayce, can you give me a hand to get her to her feet?" Ned called. He'd finished taking Mary's blood pressure and listening to her chest. Galloway and I watched as the two paramedics lifted her to her feet, made sure she was steady on her legs before handing her over to Young and Walsh. They immediately arrested her and slapped on a set of cuffs. It was almost worth getting shot for. Almost.

Ned approached, a grin on his face. "You all set for your ride?" He asked. "We'll even let you choose. You can walk out to the ambulance, or I'll get the stretcher?"

"Pft. I can walk. Honestly, it's just a flesh wound, Jayce said so himself. A couple of stitches."

"Come on then." Gathering up their gear, I followed the paramedics out to the ambulance, Galloway with a supporting arm around my waist. Not that I needed it. But it was nice, just the same.

"One more question, and we're good to go." Ned settled me onto the stretcher in the back and strapped the seatbelt over me. Galloway took a seat by my head.

"What's that?" I asked.

"Lights and sirens?"

"Guys, it's like you don't even know me." I grinned. "Lights and sirens all the way."

Get your copy of book four, *A Ghost of a Chance*, here: www.JaneHinchey.com/GhostofaChance

Thank you for reading! If you enjoyed this book, I'd greatly appreciate your review.

You can find a complete list of my books, including series and reading order on my website at:

www.JaneHinchey.com

Join my newsletter here:

www.JaneHinchey.com/ghostly-newsflash

And finally, join my readers group on Facebook here:

www.JaneHinchey.com/LittleDevils

Thank you so much for taking a chance and reading my book . It's readers like you who make this journey worthwhile and fuel my passion for storytelling. Your support means the world to me, and I can't wait to share more exciting stories with you in the future.

xoxo
Jane

Are you a fan of the Ghost Detective mysteries? Sign up for my newsletter and receive two bonus Ghost Detective shorts!

www.janehinchey.com/ghostly-newsflash

READ MORE BY JANE

Find them all at www.JaneHinchey.com/books

The Ghost Detective Mysteries

#1 Ghost Mortem

#2 Give up the Ghost

#3 The Ghost is Clear

#4 A Ghost of a Chance

#5 Here Ghost Nothing

#6 Who Ghost There?

#7 Wild Ghost Chase

#8 Easy Come, Easy Ghost

#9 Life Ghost On

Witch Way Paranormal Cozy Mystery Series

#1 Witch Way to Magic & Mayhem

#2 Witch Way to Romance & Ruin

#3 Witch Way Down Under

#4 Witch Way to Beauty & the Beach

#5 Witch Way to Death & Destruction

#6 Witch Way to Secrets & Sorcery

<u>The Gravestone Mysteries</u>

#1 Fur the Hex of it

#2 Battle of the Hexes

#3 What the Hex

<u>The Midnight Chronicles</u>

#1 One Minute to Midnight

#2 Two Minutes Past Midnight

#3 Third Strike of Midnight

<u>Clean Scene Inc.</u>

#1 All in Vein

PARANORMAL ROMANCE/URBAN FANTASY

The Awakening Trilogy

Hell's Angel Trilogy

The Enforcer Series (4 books)

Standalones

Returned

Secret Fates

Destiny's Touch

Blood Cursed

Heart of Darkness

ABOUT JANE

Hi there! I'm Jane, crafting tales of paranormal cozy mysteries sprinkled with urban fantasy romance. Between sips of coffee and dodging my mischievous cats, I immerse myself in stories where magic meets everyday life.

Once known as Zahra Stone in the world of steamy urban fantasy, I've now merged those fiery tales under the Jane Hinchey banner. Off the page you'll find me binging on true crime documentaries or sneaking in a Power Nap. Dive into my stories and join me on an enchanting journey!

Find me here: www.janehinchey.com

facebook.com/janehincheyauthor

instagram.com/janehincheyauthor

amazon.com/Jane-Hinchey/e/B0193449MI

bookbub.com/authors/jane-hinchey

goodreads.com/jane_hinchey

www.ingramcontent.com/pod-product-compliance
Lightning Source LLC
Chambersburg PA
CBHW050148120726
47903CB00002B/542